Humaning

By
S. Coop

Kinfolk Books
Roanoke, VA

Cover art courtesy of INCO Designs
Edited by JJ Murray

PUBLISHER'S NOTE
This is a work of fiction. Names, characters, places, and incidents either are the product of the author's imagination and experiences or are used fictitiously, and any resemblance to actual persons, living or dead, events, or locales is entirely coincidental.

Special thanks to my family and my friends, my editor, JJ Murray, and to you readers, old and new, who have given me a chance to show you a little of what goes on in the mind of S. Coop!

Humaning

Prologue

I am flawed, but my intentions are good … usually. I've lived a long time—a very long time—and what I've learned is that humans are what they are. There is nothing special nor different about most of them. They will be evil or kind—with no in between. How and what a human becomes is simply in his or her blood. Their DNA tells me everything I need to know about them. Their blood is their interpreter, and it sings a song only I can hear.

Their last song, so to speak.

Blood is something that has consumed my life—my immortal life. I've lived on this earth for over two millennia and I have yet to evolve into something that needs no blood. However, my thirst has decreased, but with that came a catch. Isn't that usually the case? You get the bad with the good? Never just the good. Who knows, maybe in another two thousand years I will be able to walk the earth needing nothing at all but living that much longer is not appealing nor is it a goal of mine.

Given the circumstances, would I say I'm a good man? No, I'm not a good man, but I am a good *monster*. I could be a hell of a lot worse. The thing is, I don't exist to feed or prey on humans. I exist purely for love. Period. My identity is my secret until I want to share it. It's better that way. I love being a mystery.

However, there is one thing I do envy about humans, and that is most live without ever bothering to learn more than what is right in front of them. It's willful ignorance at its best. Sounds like a stress-free life if you ask me.

But I get to see it all—the good, the bad, and the insanely ugly! I've lived long enough to look at ignorance as a gift. Tunnel vision and rose-colored glasses are my ultimate goals.

I am vastly different than any creature that has ever existed. I am a hybrid of sorts. I have one vampiric ability which is drinking blood, coupled with an unknown. My shifting power is due to an amalgamation of things thrown together to create me. I'm certain of it. There is no name for what I am.

I'm basically a paranormal mutt.

When I said I needed blood, I meant it. I no longer crave it or get a taste for it, but I literally need it to survive. I am a mystery wrapped in a riddle cooked on high heat and based with a conundrum.

That's how mysterious I am.

Hell, I'm still somewhat a mystery to myself, but one thing I can say is that I don't like to be a mystery to her. My Sera. I wish she knew who I was ... who *she* was. She is the only thing that matters—even after all this time. She has seen a lot, too, but she doesn't remember the bad. She can't help but forget. I don't blame her.

I first met Sera when she was an impressionable 26-year-old woman, and I was thirty-three. That was in my mortal life. Now she is stuck in a perpetual merry-go-round of reincarnation. Why is she coming back? Well, that's my fault, so the least I can do is be here while she goes through it. I have come to the conclusion that there is only one thing that will set her free—set *us* free. And ... that is inevitably death. *Real death.*

I haven't looked for her in half a century and that's because whenever I see her, we connect, then she dies. Usually right in front of me. Seeing her die over and over takes a toll on me, so I take a break sometimes. I have to.

My absence varies from centuries to decades, then to years. Often, I get off the ride and regroup. Alas, I return to this tragic path, and I am a glutton for punishment.

What can I say? I'm a melancholy dude. What I've realized through all these years is that I *thrive* off love and the tragedy it brings. It makes this existence bearable. If you're thinking a person changes dramatically when they become immortal, then you would be wrong. It's basically the same—minus the whole blood drinking and shifting thing.

There is always one thing that remains the same in all Sera's lives, and that's literature. It is what pulled us together in the first place. She is always drawn to it—hence, she is trying to draw near me and doesn't even know it.

So, I'm back again, hopefully for the last time.

This will be the thirteenth time I've found her.

Lucky 13.

S. Coop

The human race has improved everything but the human race.
-Adlai E. Stevenson

1

Léoan

It's her day to work. She's scheduled four days a week, with alternating weekends. Yes, I know it sounds creepy and stalker-ish that I know this, but she's mine and always has been. There's no debating that.

Tonight is a special night. I found her a month ago and tonight I am finally going to introduce myself. I love when she works at night. I don't have to get out in the daytime. Don't get me wrong, I am able to go out in the day, I just prefer not to. I don't particularly like humans. I just tolerate them and use them when I need to.

There she is. I see her walk through the double doors of the library entrance. She's wearing a pink flower-patterned scarf and black ankle boots. I wonder why she wears boots to work. She stands on her feet the entire shift, but she does have nice calves to show for it. Black tights run up and down her legs tucking themselves perfectly into those boots, and an oversized tan sweater hugs her torso. She's not one for color and is usually dressed in black from head to toe, giving off that Metal vibe. Or is it Emo? It's always changing from decade to decade, but what gets me every time I see her is her hair. I play this little game, guessing what it's going to look like next, and I wait with bated breath to see if I'm correct. Will it be kinky? Will it be straight? Will she wear braids or locks? Yes, I know all the hair jargon. I read it on the internet.

This body she's occupying is the closest she's ever come to Sera. Breathtaking—just as she always was. It is as if she teleported to this time.

Lifting a *Time Magazine* to my face, I peek around the side. She's working at the counter today, which means she will have to smile. That's something she doesn't do much. I plan to change that. It will be just like old times. Just me and her. Except this time, things will be different. This time I won't get caught slipping.

After thumbing through a few more pages, I notice she's moved from the counter to putting books on the shelves. And she's *sooo* close to me. I breathe in the aroma of her body spray. It's nothing expensive, but it's fruity, strawberry to be exact. So sweet, just like her.

This is the moment of truth. I set the magazine down and straighten out my thick, gray Aran sweater as if it has wrinkles in it. I'm feeling a little nervous. Meeting the love of your life is never easy. I've done it twelve times before. You would think I'd be a pro at it by now. I clear my throat. Here goes nothing.

"Excuse me, Miss?" I say.

She turns to me with bloodshot eyes.

What is going on here? I look at her nametag. "Samia Greysen?"

"Umm." She wipes her face. "Yes? Can I help you?"

"Are you okay?" I ask. She's not supposed to be like this. She's supposed to look at me and we instantly connect. She's not here. She's not here with me and we are not connecting!

The sides of her lips curl upwards. "Yes, thank you. Just bad allergies."

"Pesky things," I reply. She's lying. She is not okay.

We stand there in silence. The vibe has to hit her eventually. Hey! It's me! The love of your life, or lives! The

one and only thing you can't live without! Instead of that happening, she looks at me expectantly.

"The Odyssey?"

"Homer?" she replies.

I briefly close my eyes and breathe in and out. Music to my ears. I open my eyes to her waving the book back and forth in my face, sniffing. How did she do that so quickly?

She points to the shelf right next to me. "Have you read the Iliad? It's his first."

Of course, I'm standing right by it! I didn't think that one through. Hmm...have I read it? Yes, I have. As a matter of fact, I am very familiar with it.

Her nosy boss, Nancy, calls her from the front counter. Every time I come here, she stares at me as if she knows me. I really dislike her. I watch as Samia leaves me and walks over to her. *Damnit!* I didn't even introduce myself. I've lost my touch. It's never been this hard before.

She settles behind the counter, propping herself up on a chair in front of a computer screen. I walk up to the counter, set the book down, and slide my library card over while looking into her beautiful, normally vibrant, and expressive umber eyes. Long eyelashes hover over them, protecting anyone from getting in. But I see. Sadness is written all over them. *Why are you so sad, my love?*

"Léoan? Lee-awn?" she says, snapping me out of my daze. "Is that how you pronounce your first name?"

"It's pronounced like 'lay own.' Sort of like 'lay it own' me." I chuckle but she doesn't.

Smooth.

"Your last name is Onassis? Like Jackie O?"

"Correct." I smile. She puts the book under the scanner, and a red line appears over the numerical tag, followed by a loud beep.

"That's a very unique name," she says.

"It's Greek, mostly. The last name is."

She gives me back my card, then hands me a receipt that tells me when the book is due back. "You're good to go, Lay-own."

I stare at her like a deer in headlights. "Oh, of course!" I pick up the book and head toward the exit, then turn around for one last glimpse of her until I come again. And ... she's not there.

Samia

ALMOST THREE YEARS OF MY LIFE I WASTED WITH him. He knew I was vulnerable when we met. He promised he wouldn't hurt me! I angrily scroll down my ex's new girlfriend's Facebook page. Oh, look at that. She's already changed her last name to his. We broke up two weeks ago! That bastard! I gave him a chance when I had doubts about him. I trusted him and he leaves me for this…this…who knows what it is! Where is her hairline! I went to her as a woman and she mocked me. Well, have fun with a cheating, broke piece of shit, ma'am!

"What you lookin' at?" Kristen, my co-worker and very best friend asks me as she rounds the corner into the sorting room. Before I can click out of the page, she grabs the phone. "Is … is that her?"

I nod.

"She looks…interesting."

"I know. Apparently, he has a thing for women with edge deficiency."

Kristen laughs. "You make it sound like a medical condition. If you've been hurt and someone has snatched your edges, please give us a call at 1-800-I-Need-Edges "

"Speaking of edges. Please tell me you didn't use glue with that." I point to her wig.

"No, I did not use glue, but I have to wear this wig because Miss Cruella doesn't like my current hair color, and it seems whatever she says goes around here even though she's only a step above us in the hierarchy."

"I do like the blonde though."

"Thank you, dawling," she poses with her best southern drawl.

I giggle through the pain for a moment. "You know, I don't think I was hood enough for him. He would make comments here and there about how 'white' I act. I should have known he was trash from the start. I mean, he still listens to R Smelly. Plus, he's obsessed with NWA. Who in their right mind is obsessed with those guys? I swear he thinks he's a 1980's gangster pimp."

"Well, he's a wigger, that's for sure."

I shake my head because Kristen has absolutely no filter. She's beautiful, perky, and unique but gives approximately zero fucks about offending anybody.

"Girl, what? Wiggers are the worst. I refuse to date them and I'm white! They've all got this warped sense of what being black is and it usually ain't it. Besides, it's a good thing he did this now. Imagine if y'all had gotten married or you became his baby mama or something."

"Ace said he doesn't want kids."

"I'm sure he told you he didn't want to do a lot of things, yet here he is doing them."

I take the phone back and look at her name again and my heart drops to the pit of my stomach. "Please tell me to dox him! I want all his information plastered all over the internet. Nudes and everything. He's got a lot of enemies that would love that information.

"No! Absolutely not! We are going out this weekend, and you're going to find yourself a play toy. Just watch, you will be over him before you know it."

I look at her but stay silent. How wrong she is right now. I've never loved anyone the way I love Ace. She doesn't understand how serious we were. Apparently, he didn't either.

"I'm back," Nancy says, coming in from her smoke break smelling like Marlboro Reds and failure. "We need those books back on the shelf." She points to a cart I was working on earlier.

Well, I was doing that before you interrupted me to cover for you!

I wheel the cart back to the shelves and start putting books back and instantly start to tear up ... again. I really thought Ace was "The One." We spent every waking moment together for almost three years until he got a new job. Then he hardly had time for me. Turns out, he was making time for someone else. It's extremely hard going to work with a broken heart. It's taking everything I have in me not to walk right out of those doors and go home to lick my wounds. But this is my dream job. Something about being surrounded by books comforts me. It's quiet and everything seems to go in slow motion. In a way, it's my sanctuary—*my bubble*. I can cry here and get away with it. I used to believe you could cry someone out of your system, but I don't know about that anymore. Giving someone your heart after swearing off love is a huge step to take. I stepped out of that box but got punched back in it.

"Break time. Go take your fifteen." Nancy eyes me.

Do you want these books up or not! Geez, make up your mind woman!

I push the cart back to the sorting area, grab my notebook from my locker, and head upstairs to the break room. No one's here. I sigh with relief. This is another reason I love to work nights. No pretense, no fake attempt at being "social" with co-workers. I can just be me. My own little quiet self.

I get on my Facebook and scroll down Ace's page There they are, hugged up together happy and smiling. The cheating asshole and the homewrecker. Must be nice to smile. I don't think I've smiled in two weeks. At least, not a genuine smile. Smiling is overrated anyway. I study the picture harder. He does look handsome, and that makes me even angrier.

She's fallen for him, but he's definitely a wolf in sheep's clothing. I'll just wait on the side and watch as everything falls apart. How can anyone be so happy after making another person so miserable? Sounds like a great recipe for karma. I am almost certain once that woman looks past what's on his outside, she won't like what's on the inside. I'll bank on that. She's too shallow to love the crust of him. The awkward, the wrong, the goofiness, and his shortcomings. She loves the exterior, and exteriors are only beautiful for so long.

I start writing in my notebook and soon, it's time to go back to work. These breaks fly by so damn fast! I get up and drag myself to the elevator. Once in, I close the doors, h t the emergency stop, and sit down, bringing my knees up and resting my head on them, I hug my shins and sob.

2

Léoan

~~~~~~~~~~

Samia pulls out of the library parking lot after everyone else has left. She shouldn't do that. There could be anyone waiting around watching her. I cross the street and get into my own car and sit and pause for a second, letting her turn the corner before I start mine and follow. I already know the route, so there's no need to stick too close to her. I think about how I approached her earlier and how absolutely nothing went as planned.

Was it the way I looked? I guess, maybe I looked too buttoned up? Too serious? I wanted to make a good "first" impression. Who wouldn't want to look his absolute best when meeting his soulmate? Next time, I think I'll dress more relaxed.

I'm playing all these thoughts through my head when I realize I have yet to really get to know her. I've been watching her, and I've noticed that she possesses all the mannerisms of Sera. There are some differences and those are the things I need to know. I need to dig deep and really get to know *this* her. With every new life, there is a new personality. So, I must get to know hers, but to do that, I must get her somewhere that I can *get* to know her. A date, perhaps? Yes! Perfect. Now, I only have to get her to agree to one, which at this point isn't looking too promising.
~~~~~~~~~~

As I watch her pull into her assigned parking space and go inside her apartment, my vision goes blurry. I shake it off, in an attempt to clear it up.

It gets better, the fog clears, but I know that it's past time to replenish. This is the part that I hate. I was hoping this time would last longer than usual. Although two weeks in exchange for three months isn't a bad trade. I suppose it could be worse. Hell, I used to have to replenish much more frequently than now. Evolution has been partly on my side, so I can't really complain.

When I get to my apartment, I change into my boxers and hop online to scroll down Samia's page. She accepted my request from a female burner account. I know she wouldn't accept me otherwise because she is very much to herself. All this time, I had no idea she was dating him. That's how private she is. I could have been better prepared had I known this. I scroll down her page and land on a poem she posted a few hours ago.

Counterfeit Beauty

You saved me
To kill me
I suppose you were the one who
Wanted to drive a dagger through my heart
Is victory as sweet as you thought?
Do you sleep with her in your arms?
Does she know you slew a dragon with your charm?
Like a snake, you shed your skin
Leaving a molten pile of shit, lies, and disappointment
Do you swallow proudly knowing you're tricky?
And does she know you're a wolf in sheep's clothing?
Is she mesmerized by your counterfeit beauty?
Innocent, candid, driven and naïve
That was not you

I saw what you wanted me to see
And I believed
Bravo! Good looking!
It's quite the accomplishment
That I let you in
But
Never, EVER again...

Yikes! So, this is why she's upset. Whoever this guy is, he really did a number on her. I want to know who is occupying her thoughts. I want to know who is keeping her blind to me. This person has caused her so much pain. It will be hard to get to her if she's broken-hearted and in love with someone.

I see a comment from Kristen pop up under the post.

Kristen Fox Ace is a piece of shit. You deserve better!

Ace who? I sit and ponder how I can find this guy's page. There's got to be millions of Aces in North Carolina. I'm sure that isn't his real name, but I have to track him down.

I open the messaging app, and a dick pic immediately pops up. Why do men do this? I feel sorry for the women who go through this shit on a daily basis. I've got enough dick pics in here to last two lifetimes. I guess it doesn't help that I chose an incredibly attractive woman from a stock photo site for my profile picture. A little reverse image search and I would be found out, but that probably doesn't matter to them as the only thing they seem to use the internet for is sending unsuspecting women their unimpressive junk.

I crack my knuckles in anticipation of the investigating I will be doing to find this guy's page. I type in North Carolina in the location field and type Ace. I scroll through about six when I see someone named King Ace that looks to be about Samia's age.

Clicking the page, the first thing I notice is that he's got tons of stuff public. Tons of photos with him and his friends at clubs and photos of him performing at what looks like hole in the wall joints. There are heaps of selfies and not one picture of Samia. "There's got to be more." I request a few people off his page and then request him after they accept. It looks more legitimate if we have mutuals. Once he accepts me, I look through what he doesn't have on public and I finally see one picture where Samia tagged him.

Bingo.

I see the pictures of him and a woman who is far from attractive. This must be the new victim.

Just as I'm being nosy, blurriness hits me again only this time, I can't get it to clear. I sit up on my bed, holding my head, trying to steady myself when I collapse on the floor and into darkness.

TWO HOURS LATER I WAKE IN A PUDDLE OF SWEAT.

"Fuck! I'm so tired of this shit!"

I crawl to the kitchen and reach up to open the fridge. Grabbing a gallon of spare blood for emergencies, I chug it with a fervor of an alcoholic devouring a can of beer. I usually warm it up because it's more pleasant, but I'm in no shape to be picky. I need just enough to get by, not enough to change.

I lie down and look up at the ceiling. My sight comes back—*slightly*—and a little energy returns to my body. I crawl to the bathtub and run water over myself, washing away the ickiness and I'm feeling much better, but this will only last me an hour, tops. I hate it, but I must fix myself. I waited too long. I should have known that going over three months would result in this mess.

I get out of the bathtub, slowly stand, and look at myself in the mirror. A sweaty, pale face stares back at me. My hair is disheveled with dripping wet black curls dangling over my eyes, and I realize I'm in dire need of a cut. I use my hand and lazily slick it back. That ought to last five minutes. Walking back into my room, I see the puddle on the floor and I flinch. I should have known better, but finding Sera threw off my timing. I had to see her as myself and nobody else, so I waited. Seems totally logical but stupid at the same time.

I toss on a fresh pair of blue jeans and a T-shirt, followed by a ball cap and trench coat. I'm sure I don't look suspicious at all. I grab my keys and race out the door.

Picking a target takes precision. Over the years I've been able to pinpoint specific people—those who won't be missed if they suddenly were to *disappear*. I'm doing society a favor most of the time. Have I killed people that I probably shouldn't have killed? Of course, I have, but shit happens.

"No Man's Land" is a little hellhole part of town known for drugs, prostitution, gangs, and violence—the perfect place for nefarious dealings. After finding a parking spot, I hop out of my car and walk down the street, being sure to pull my ball cap down over my face as much as possible. I swear I feel like Nosferatu when I do this.

I'm passing down an alley when I see a man knocking the shit out of a woman there.

"Bitch! I warned you not to steal from me! You made twenty more dollars than this. Give it here!" He smacks her in the face again.

"I swear, that's all I got!" she sobs, her mascara racing down her pale, sunken-in cheeks.

He pulls out a gun, holds it to her head, and cocks it back. "Bitch, I'm erasing you! Lyin' ass hoe—"

I charge him before he can pull the trigger, running him up against the brick of the building he's standing beside, knocking him out cold. I motion to the woman, "Leave!" She gathers up her money and complies, crying and looking back as she makes her escape in six-inch heels. She won't talk.

I take my jacket off and kneel next to Mr. Pimp. Hmm, dreads, glasses. I guess it won't be so bad.

He wakes up. "What the fuck—"

Kneeling beside him, I get to work just as he wakes up. "Hey, sleepy head. I would say sorry for what I'm about to do, but I'm gonna take a wild guess and say that you're an asshole, so, I'm really *not* sorry." I start pulling his clothes off. I always do this. I'm six foot four so my victims are usually never my size anyway.

"Get away from me you crazy muthafucka! Stooooop!" he screams at the top of his lungs.

"Please. It's much easier if I do this now. It's so much harder to do when you're a stiff corpse."

"Look in my pockets. I've got money. Take it and let me go...please."

"I don't want your money. Besides, you were about to kill someone over money. How much money can you possibly have if you're that hard up for twenty dollars?" I reach into his pocket and pull out a tattered knock-off Gucci wallet. It's made pretty well and can fool someone who doesn't know better, and lo and behold it's empty! *I knew it.* I pull out his ID card. "Montrell Thomas."

"Help!" he screams.

I put my hand over his mouth and say calmly, "Don't. Do. That. Montrell." I shake my head. "I mean, help me out here, man."

"Mmmmmmmmm," he groans.

"What?" I put my ear to his mouth. "I can't hear you and neither can anyone else."

"Mmmmmmmmmmmmmmmm!" he yells against my hand.

I sigh. He's not a good listener and he's so frightened. Devastated! His heart is beating a mile a minute. Who can live with this kind of trauma? I'll be doing him a favor. Oh, enough already. Don't need anyone coming by, seeing this, and trying to be a hero. *I'm* the hero here. I'm getting rid of the bad guy.

Biting into his jugular and draining him of every ounce of blood he possesses gives me the anecdote my body needs. However temporary that may be. His body goes cold and turns gray as I'm depleting him of life and I'm relieved that he is no longer talking. When I'm finished I back away as the metamorphosis begins. I feel the blood run through my deprived veins, filling them and plumping them up. I'm feeling so much better already. I look at my arms and see the beginnings of my new form. My skin transforms from its porcelain to a deep coffee-colored tone. I feel my hair grow past my shoulders, coiling into thick dreads. It only takes a few minutes until the transformation is complete.

After the deed is done, I look around and everything is blurry, not because I'm in need of sustenance, but because that motherfucker was blind as shit! I take his glasses and plop them onto my nose. That's better. I grab the remainder of his clothes, dress and get ready to leave as Ms. Six-inch heels comes back, shaking and cautiously approaching me. She sees her used to be pimp lying dead on the ground and his doppelganger—me— standing next to him.

"Oh, my God!" she yells as she backs away.

I catch her before she makes it to the main street. "I thought I told you to leave. You're such a lovely woman, and I don't want to have to do to you what I did to him. Okay?"

She nods.

"You didn't see this. None of this. You don't know what happened here, do you?'

"No." she replies, still trembling.

"Great! You are a nice lady. Go home and change your life. No more selling your body or doing drugs. Go to school, get an education, and live your best life. Got it?"

"Yes," she smiles.

Charming humans is not a vampiric ability I gained. Over centuries I have become an expert in bending folks to my will simply by using good old-fashioned charm. It's not one-hundred percent foolproof, but I get by.

I leave her standing there. I'm sure she'll do great.

WHEN I WALK THROUGH MY DOOR, MY CROTCH STARTS burning. It feels like a thousand fire ants are having a party in my pants.

"Ugh!" I get to the bathroom and take down my pants and underwear to see my dick covered with sores, oozing thick white liquid.

Two weeks of this shit! Fuck me!

It happens. This isn't the first time I had to deal with a disease the human I drained possessed. It will all go away soon enough. I sigh with relief. I couldn't imagine a lifetime of crotch rot. I get undressed and a tube of Aloe vera falls out of my pants pocket.

Aloe vera it is. I wonder if it ever occurred to him to go to the doctor? I shake my head as I run freezing cold bath water.

As I'm soaking in the water, I wonder what Samia is doing right now. Probably crying over that jerk! Ace the dick is such a prick! He left you for a trick! Not my best, but at least it rhymes. I have once again lost the will to write. It's way past writer's block. My ability to write is sitting on the other side of a poisonous snake covered cement wall. There are spikes there, too. Big, thick spikes the snakes are slithering around.

After hopping out of the tub, I slather the Aloe vera over the sores. Oh my God, that feels so good. My eyes roll to the back of my head. Maybe he was on to something. But still, he should have really gotten this taken care of. Now I have to deal with it. Some people are so inconsiderate.

I shrug and lie on my bed and see the faint glow of lights through the blinds. It's almost daytime, but it's not a big deal. One good thing about my condition is that I can go out in the sun for as long as I want. I think I'll visit the library again soon. At least this way I won't seem like a creepy stalker because I will be in a different body. It's a win, win, of course, minus the STI.

Now, let me put this body to good use.

3

Samia

Kristen picks me up at ten p.m. sharp. I finally agreed to go out somewhere with her. I don't particularly feel like going, but she insisted this would help me "get over that asshole." I look in my closet and decide to spice it up tonight and grab a pair of black, pleather tights and a low-cut top with designs cut out on the back and short sleeves. Sexy, but still leaves something to the imagination. I blow dry my hair and smooth the sides up, using combs to hold it in place as I make a Frohawk. Edgy with a side of femininity. Last but not least, I put on a full face of makeup and add a touch of highlighter to my upper cheeks, tip of my nose, my chin, and cupids bow. Just one last thing. I wrap a black, studded choker around my neck. Looking at myself in the mirror, I am impressed. It's been a long time since I've gone to a club. Might as well do it big.

Kristen pulls up and honks her horn. I quickly throw on black ankle boots with buckles on the side. I'm not wearing heels. I want to be able to dance and not feel like my feet are going to fall off at the end of the night. I go outside, walking unenthusiastically, and get in the passenger seat of Kristen's twilight-purple Chevy Camaro convertible, one of the cars her many sugar daddies recently bought her.

"Lookin' good, girl!" she says as she turns up the music and hands me a lit joint.

"Really?" I shake my head.

"What?" She looks at me as if she has no idea what I'm talking about.

"You're supposed to be the designated driver, yet here you are getting high before we even get to the club."

"Girl, you know I got a high tolerance." She shoves the joint at me again.

I'm going to end up in jail messing with her. I take a small puff, inhaling only half of what I sucked. Ten minutes later I'm feeling high as a kite while we make the drive to Muse Nightclub. Kristen lets the top down, and the cool air hits me. She then looks at me and giggles, her lavender hair with purple roots dancing wildly in the wind.

"How do you feel?" she asks, knowing I'm already higher than gas prices.

"I'm good," I say, and I'm not lying. I am good, good. "I think I just saw a pink unicorn pass by. It was beautiful."

"Damn, how long has it been since you had some loud?"

"Since the last time you forced me to smoke some," I reply.

When we get to Muse Nightclub, Kristen pulls into the valet parking, and we get out of the car. She hands the attendant her keys while winking at him. "Take care of her. I worked hard for this bitch."

The young attendant shakes his head and pulls off, spinning out as he leaves.

"I know he didn't! There better not be one scratch on her when he brings her back!" Kristen is pissed with a "I'm gonna talk to your manager" look on her face.

I can't help but laugh. Had she not told him all that, he probably wouldn't have driven it like a stunt driver in Fast and Furious.

Muse Nightclub is an upscale club where wealthy and the want-to-be wealthy party. I stick out like a sore thumb in this place. I'm dressed in Punk Chic while most of the other patrons are dressed in Instagram fabulous. Like robots, they are snapping selfies and making duck lips while doing any and everything. Sipping a drink? Snap! Jamming to music? Snap! Breathing? Snap, snap, snap!

Like any club around this time, there is already a drunk girl on top of one of the tables dancing with a way too short dress on and men standing around ogling and egging her on. Where are her friends? They're probably just as wasted as she is. I am not getting white girl wasted like that. No way!

We go to the bar that's lined with blue and purple neon lights with a surface that's littered with confetti. Kristen puts in an order for the strongest shots they have, which doesn't surprise me one bit. She hands me a glass, we clink them together, and then down them. That burns. After three more of those, I am on that very table with said girl!

"Wooooo hoooooo! Fuck yeah!"

White girl wasted.

After a few moments, Kristen pulls me down and drags me over to a table where two guys are sitting. "Mia, this is Scott." She points to a guy with sandy blond hair strewn up into a messy man bun. "And this is Jacob." She points to a guy with mocha-colored skin and a huge beard that refuses to connect to his mustache.

Typical hipster douches, but for good measure, I introduce myself to both of them. Scott squeezes my hand a little too hard when he shakes it, and Jacob barely looks up from his phone long enough to be cordial. So, I plop down next to Scott and we chat. He's boring. Extremely boring, and my mind drifts back to Ace. This little outing was supposed to make me forget about him, but it seems to have done the opposite.

A waitress comes by, and Scott orders a round of shots while Jacob flirts with her, then looks at me and smirks as if I know him and I give a fuck that he's flirting. Then he decides to speak to me and neg me. "I like the whole Chaka Khan thing you got going on. Not really my taste but it's unique."

"Thanks, I say. "Have you ever thought of using any Miracle Grow on your moustache so that it connects with your beard? It looks like it's trying to run away from your face." I tilt my head and smile at him.

Scott laughs, and some of his drink goes shooting out of his nose. "Dammmnnnn!"

"Man fuck that trick," Jacob barks.

I shrug. "What the fuck did I do?"

"Okay, everybody let's cool down," Kristen interjects. "You don't have to be a dick," she blasts Jacob.

"Fuck you. too!" he snaps at her.

Kristen narrows her eyes and stares at him. I can tell she's about to snap. Scott puts his arm around her and whispers in her ear. Whatever he's saying instantly calms her.

Jacob shakes his head and looks back down at his phone while I motion to Kristen for us to go to the bathroom. She's not looking at me because she's talking to Scott, who is all over her now. I decide to go by myself, so I get up, barely holding my composure, and go on a toilet-seeking adventure. I'm in a drunken haze and everything is moving in slow motion as I manage to dart around the crowd and make my way to the bathroom, which to my dismay is occupied, of course. I lean against the wall and wait, wishing there was somewhere to sit before I pass out.

"So, you don't like my beard?" Jacob shows up out of nowhere.

I look at him and roll my eyes.

He gets close to me so that our faces are mere inches away. "I got something I know you will like." He pushes up against me, and I can feel his hard penis poking my stomach. I try to push him away, but he's too strong. He laughs, reaches around, and grabs one of my butt cheeks.

"Come on, Mami. You know you want—"

Suddenly, Jacob gets snatched away, taking me on the trip with him. I go tumbling to the floor as I see a man reaching over me and picking Jacob up by the throat. That's when I black out.

WHEN I WAKE UP, I'M AT KRISTEN'S APARTMENT LYING ON the couch.

"The dead has risen."

I rub my eyes and look through the blur to see Scott standing there in a pink bathrobe. Sitting up, I look around.

"Don't worry, Jacob isn't here. Sorry about what happened."

I give Scott a dirty look. "Your friend is an asshole."

"Hey, we work together. He's not a douche at work. That Uber driver whooped his ass good, though. Jacob left the club on a stretcher."

"Yeah, I've never seen a pimp hand that strong," Kristen says. "He choked and slapped the living shit out of Jacob. It was hilarious."

"Uber driver?" I furrow my eyebrows.

"Apparently the one you called after you snuck off to the bathroom." Kristen goes to the kitchen then returns with a cup of coffee and sets it on the table in front of me.

"I called an Uber?"

"Yes, and I'm actually glad you did because none of us were in any condition to drive," she says.

I give her an "I told you so" look. "Remind me to never go out with you again."

She gives me a guilty look.

"Ugh, and we have to work tonight! How am I supposed to get home?"

"Scott pulled some strings and had it brought here."

After taking a sip of the bitter liquid, I almost spit it out. "Umm, you know I like heavy on the cream, light on the coffee."

"Oh, hush. This will help your hangover."

My phone rings, and it's Ace. I go into Kristen's bathroom and answer it. "What?" I do my best to sound unenthusiastic.

"Hey."

I stay silent.

"I know you're mad at me, but we need to talk."

"About?" I ask in an overtly smart-ass tone. Must still be the alcohol talking. This is what I've been wanting, right? Still, I have to act like this isn't what I've been wanting.

"About us," he replies.

"I don't think that's a good idea," I say.

"Please, baby. Just give me a chance to explain things. I know you're hurt. Let me fix what I messed up. I'm so sorry." I hear a sniffle from his end of the phone.

He's crying? Ace is crying? He's not playing fair. "I don't know, I will have to see. I have to work today."

"Please think about it, hard," he begs, followed by another sniffle. "I miss you."

Click. I hang up on him. He needs to feel like he's lost me. He needs to feel unsure for once in his damn life. He's lucky I'm even talking to him at all. Hmph!

I come out of the bathroom, and Scott is shoving his tongue down Kristen's throat.

"Please take me home when y'all are done playing tonsil hockey."

4

Léoan

It's taken me a week to get used to this body. This dude had more problems than I previously thought. He had to have eaten and smoked like he had absolutely nothing to lose. I couldn't last five minutes on the treadmill, but I still beat the shit out of that asshole that was assaulting Samia. At least, I could do that much.

Usually, when I occupy a body, I like to make the time I'm in it as seamless as possible. That being eating better and keeping fit. I take a risk becoming human because there is a huge possibility that if I do happen to die while in human form, I may die for good. I'm not sure, I haven't tested that theory, nor do I want to at this particular time. I need to be here for Samia. She will determine when I leave this earth.

I brush my teeth and shave this God-awful beard Montrell sported. That's better. I look at my appearance. Meh, could be worse. I throw on my trench and head out the door and get to the library at five p.m. sharp. As I'm walking to the entrance, I see my reflection and realize I look like the Predator. Great.

Walking inside, I see Samia at the front counter, scanning books someone is checking out, so I find a comfy table in the corner next to the adult fiction section but still in view of her. I grab a book and start reading, all the while keeping an eye on her. She looks better today. She's got a pep in her step. A night on the town did her some good. She must finally be getting over that asshole.

Once I'm myself again, it will be prime time to shoot my shot. And I never miss. That thought makes me giddy, and this book *is really* great. It's about a newly divorced man on a trip to find himself after 50 years of marriage. Fifty years! Wow—

"Montrell?"

I almost jump out of my seat. I turn around and see Samia standing there. Holy shit!

"How have you been? I haven't seen you since high school. How are you holding up?" She hits me with a barrage of questions.

"I, um. I'm holding up pretty good." I play it cool because I have no fucking idea what she's talking about.

"I'm sorry for your loss. I know you've probably heard this from a lot of folks, but it will get better. I couldn't imagine what I would do if I lost my dad."

"Yeah, my dad was my best friend. My mom is still heartbroken about it."

She gives me a confused look while I dig myself in a deeper hole. "I mean, he was the backbone of the family, but I'm doing my part and taking care of mom while she's mourning ... and ... stuff."

"But ... I thought your mom was the one that died. You posted the obituary and everything, even pictures graveside with your dad standing there."

Fuck! "Yeah, that's ... what I meant. My mind is so scrambled from all the grief that I get my parents mixed up."

"Oh ... kay," she says.

I flip the book closed, stand up, and clear my throat. "I'm going to get this book."

"Oh," she says. "Follow me."

We get to the counter, and she puts her hand out. It looks so dainty and soft. I want to grab it and steal off into the night with her.

"Montrell?" she breaks me out of my daydream "Library card?"

"Oh!" I start fiddling through my coat and pull out my library card and set it on the counter. She looks at the card and looks up at me, confused.

Fuck. Yes, that's my library card! My library card. Not Montrell's!

'I ... must have picked up my friend's card." I say, laughing nervously. "Let me just ..." I reach for the card right as a dreadlock falls off my head and onto the counter.

"Oh my God!" she steps back, covering her mouth with her hand.

"I..." I grab the dread and race for the door, losing more as I make my way to my car.

"That was a disaster! A real clusterfuck!" I beat on the dashboard. "Ouch!" I hold my hand as the skin starts to melt away. "Not now! Not now!"

I start the car and use my elbows to steer home. I'm transforming back, but it's only been about a week! And it started at the worst fucking time as humanly possible! When I get to my apartment, leaving my teeth behind in the car, I run to the bathroom and look at myself. There is no hair, there are no teeth, and I'm molting like a snake. This is never an easy process, even after all this time. I hurry and start peeling the remaining skin off. One hell of a sunburn, I joke to myself at a time that isn't appropriate for jokes. The re-transformation is complete when my eyeballs pop out of the sockets like tennis balls being launched from a machine. They roll around in the sink before disintegrating.

The good thing about molting is that the flesh and bones turn to ash. I grab a black plastic bag and sweep the ashes up and toss them in the bag. Pulling off my clothes to shake them out, I realize I left my library card on the counter. I was too busy trying to run with hair to realize that.

I sit on the bathroom floor, tilt my head back on the wall, and beat it against it two or three times.

Perfect.

Samia

"THE WEIRDEST THING JUST HAPPENED," I SAY TO Kristen when she joins me up front.

"What?" she asks.

I show her the dreads I picked up from the floor all the way to the parking lot.

"Are you doing something new with your hair?" she asks, and I can't be mad at her because I am always doing something new with my hair, but I've never brought the hair to work un-bagged and showed it to her.

"No, this dude I know from high school dropped them. They just started falling out his head."

"Whoa, so he had a weave?"

"I think so. You know men are doing that more now. I see it on the internet all the time."

"Well, shit. He needs to get his money back."

We both laugh as I eye the library card on the counter. "Also, he left this library card."

"Okay ..." she says.

"This isn't his card. His name is Montrell. He said it was his friend's, but that name looks familiar." I read out the name

to her. "Léoan. I know this guy. Well, I don't know him, know him, but I remember who he is."

"How is that pronounced?" Kristen replies.

"Lay on, like 'Lay it own' me. That's what the guy said." I giggle. "I remember this name because it's rare, so this sure as hell isn't Montrell's card."

"Damn, so that dude's out here stealing library cards? That's low brow as fuck. Whatever happened to knocking off liquor stores?"

"Maybe stealing library cards is his kink?" I smirk.

"You never know nowadays. He probably gets off on the librarian not knowing it's really his card. Yeah, baby, scan that card."

"You know what? I'm not doing this with you today." I roll my eyes at her. "Anyway, something wasn't right, besides him losing his weave."

"He might be on that shit," she says.

"What shit?" I ask.

"I don't know, but there's always some crazy drug people do that make them do crazy stuff."

"Oh, my God, you're right. His mom just died so obviously he's not handling it well. Come to think of it he acted scared when I approached him. Maybe he was in the library because he's a homeless drug addict now? He comes from good stock, which is even sadder, but he stays in trouble. Always has."

"What a bum bitch," she says. "I'm going to shelve these books before Cruella comes out of her little broom closet and starts nagging us. I swear she watches gay porn in there."

"Eww! That's a mental image I can do without! I'm not talking about the gay porn itself. It's the thought of what she might be doing while watching it that's disturbing as fuck. Thanks a lot, Kristen."

She winks at me. "Anytime, toots."

I put the card number through, and sure enough, it pulls up Léoan Onassis. Yep. Last checked out *The Odyssey*. I wonder if he knows his library card is missing. Montrell did say they were friends, but I find that hard to believe. He's not exactly the type of guy Montrell would hang with.

I shake my head and grab my phone from under the counter and quickly go to my Facebook and pull up Montrell's page. Hmm, he hasn't posted anything in over a week. Not even a tasteless picture of him holding money. That's odd. What's this? I see several people posted on his timeline.

Tanisha Blue Montrell, where are you? You said you were bringing diapers!

Tyrone Smith Aye, where you at? HMU!

BadBaby Bree Thanks for standing me up! We are finished!

Terrell Thomas Montrell, this is your father. Call me please!

King KongLitty Yo, Wtf? Get At Me Soon As You See This, Homie.

"What is that?"

I jump as Nancy's now standing behind me with her bony hands on her hips. I put my phone down and lift up the twisted, coarse fibers. "It's hair."

"Hair?" she says.

"Yeah, a customer left it here."

"A customer left their hair here. In the library?" She looks at me with her glasses at the tip of her pointy nose.

"Pretty much." I shrug.

'Put it in the lost and found bin with a sticky note with the date and time you found it."

"What?" I chuckle. "I don't think he's coming back for this."

"You never know. Did you know him?"

"From high school but we don't really talk. I mean, I have him on social media."

"Okay, well tell him to come get it."

I roll my eyes and leave for the sorting room. Pulling out the plastic lost and found bin, I try to put the sticky note on one of the dreads. Of course, it's not sticking. I ball the note around one and shove it in there. This by far has been one of the weirdest couple of weeks. Random shit's been happening left and right but not everything has been bad. At least Ace and I are talking again.

Just as I'm thinking that, my phone vibrates. It's Ace. Speak of the devil. I look around and answer it. "Hey."

"Hey," he replies in an overly deep tone. "Are we still on for tonight?"

"Mhm," I say, keeping my voice as low as possible."

"Mhm," he mimics me, just like old times.

"I'll be out of here in about an hour."

"All right see you then," he says before hanging up.

I look around again to make sure no one saw me. If Kristen knew I was talking to Ace again, I wouldn't hear the end of it. I can't tell her yet. She hates him as much as I do …

or as much as I did. I probably shouldn't have vented to her in the first place, but she is my best friend.

The rest of the night flies by and soon, I'm on my way to meet Ace.

5

Léoan

~~~~~~~~~~

I feel much better, I breathe a sigh of relief. It's great to be me again. Like clockwork, Samia exits the library and gets in her black Toyota Highlander. She looks amazing tonight! I've never seen her wear a dress to work before. Wait. She wasn't wearing that earlier.

I start the car and follow her after she passes by me. She takes a different turn than her normal route. What's this? I speed up to get closer to her but not enough for her to catch on that I am following her. She turns into Hilltop Gate Shopping Center and parks at an Applebee's. I park and watch as she hops out of her car. Just then someone walks up to her. I get a clear look and realize it's Ace. Six foot two, pale skin and sable-colored cornrows. Yep, that's him. He s wearing black pants and a loud, yellow button up shirt that screams "I don't know how to fucking dress up."

What the hell is going on here?

They go in and are seated. I follow and request a seat behind their booth so that I'm facing Samia's back. I'm thankful the hostess is tall, so I am shielded behind her as I slide into the booth and put the menu in front of my face and listen to their conversation.

"You look fly tonight," he says.

She giggles. "Thank you. You look good. too."

She's lying. He looks like shit.
~~~~~~~~~~

"I know we've had a rough month, but I plan to make it up to you," he says.

She's silent. Could she be coming to her senses?

"Honestly, Ace, I don't know what happened between us. I've always thought we were good. I don't understand why you felt the need to look elsewhere. I had no idea you were unhappy. I let you into my life because I trusted you."

He slides in next to her on her side of the booth. "Baby, I'm sorry. It just happened. I was wrong."

"It just happened, you say. Shit doesn't just happen, Ace," she scolds him.

Tell him off! Tell him to go to hell and walk right out of this restaurant!

"Look, baby," he starts, smooth talking. "I made a huge mistake. I don't know what I was thinking or what I thought I was looking for because everything I needed was right there in front of me. I'm an idiot. If you take me back, I'll never do that again. You're the only one for me." He lifts her hand, kisses it, and caresses it. "I won't hurt you again. I promise."

What a lame excuse. She can't be buying this.

She looks down at his hand. "I did miss you."

Oh, come on!

"What can I get for you?" A waitress pounces on me. Not now! I'm trying to be nosy! "Just a sweet tea please."

"Are you waiting for someone?" she asks.

Yeah, I'm waiting for you to leave. "No, it's just going to be me." I give her a crooked smile. "I'm still looking at the food."

"Gotcha." She winks and leaves.

When she leaves my view, I hear Samia say, "Yes! I will marry you!"

No, no, no! This can't be happening. Now he's got his tongue down her throat! I want to rip his head off right here, right now! I want to wrap that yellow shirt around his neck and make his face turn every complimentary color on the color wheel! I want to launch him through the window then get in my car and run him over repeatedly! That bastard!

Alas, I sit. Feeling defeated by a guy with horrible fashion sense. I sit there quietly as the realization of losing her washes over me. I sit stuck in my own limbo, in my own karma. This is all my fault.

Before I know it, they are both leaving. I don't even bother following because I know what will happen next. They'll have makeup sex. That's usually how things work. I narrow my eyes as I watch them exit the restaurant hand in hand. They stop outside of her truck and kiss one more time, and then she leaves. I guess they are going to meet at her place. I put twenty dollars on the table and walk out. It takes everything I have in me not to fuck his world up. His phone rings as I'm unlocking my car door and I overhear him talking.

"Hey, baby."

Damn, Samia barely got out of the parking lot before she called him!

"My meeting went a little bit over. Do you know where the Applebee's is at the Hilltop?"

He's not talking to Samia. He can't be. She just left and he's already on the phone with another woman! I sit in my car and watch and wait. Ten minutes pass when a brown, rusty Toyota Corolla station wagon pulls up and a woman gets out. She's got huge tits and an even huger forehead, and on top of that, she's shaped like the letter P. She smiles at him, displaying a mouth full of teeth and gums like Mr. Ed's. I have no idea how she fits those things in her mouth.

"Hey, baby," she says, sashaying her nonexistent hips.

"Hey, sexy," he says, slapping her on her flat ass and kissing her.

So, this is what he does. Samia deserves better than this. I take out my phone, zoom in, and take pictures of them kissing. I know how much she loves Ace, and as long as she loves him, there is no chance she will ever remember how much she loved me. I hate to do this, but she has to know the truth. I get on my burner account and shoot the pictures over to Kristen via messenger. I'll let her break the news to Samia. Even if we won't be together, at least Samia won't live her life with that guy.

"Checkmate." I saltily throw my phone on the passenger seat.

IT'S BEEN A WEEK, AND I'VE BEEN WALLOWING IN enough self-pity to rival any one of Shakespeare's plays. I don't know the outcome of the pictures I sent Kristen, but I do know that Samia will need time to process everything.

I decide to return *The Odyssey* to the library. I'm not staying. Seeing how much she loves him broke my heart. Seeing her in his arms was even worse even though he is cheating on her. I go to drop the book in the chute outside the building, but it's got an out of order sign on it, so I have to walk in to return it.

Samia is not at the counter. Curiosity gets the best of me, so I walk around the library to find her. I'm passing by the teen fiction section when we run into each other.

"Excuse me." She looks up at me and apologizes with a warm smile on her face, a stack of books resting in her arms. Her eyes are beaming with light, and I'm instantly pulled in. Again.

"No problem," I say to her. She's wearing two French braids on either side of her head. She looks so cute. Cute, with just the right amount of edge.

We stare at each other and she narrows her eyes. "I think I know you."

Could this really be it? She knows who I am?

"Odyssey, right?"

"Yep. I ... just brought it back."

"I'm glad you came in."

"You are?"

"Yes. Are you missing something?"

"Missing, as in?" You, I'm missing you! Oh God, am I missing you!

"Follow me."

When we reach the front counter, she pulls out my library card. "There was a guy in here who had it. He said he was your friend. Do you know anyone named Montrell?"

"Oh ... yeah. Montrell and I go way back."

"So, you guys are friends?"

I nod.

"He left here in a very weird way and left some ... things behind."

"Oh, you know Montrell, high strung, scatter-brained at times."

"How do you know I know him?"

That's an awfully good question! I'm stumped, so of course, I lie. "I'm just speaking about how most men are in general."

"You can say that again." She giggles playfully.

"I don't know how you women deal with us. Am I right?"

She looks down, blushes, and smiles while playing with her fingers. That's when I see it. An engagement ring. My heart drops to the pit of my stomach.

"You're still engaged?" I blurt out without thinking.

She smiles widely. "Yes, I am."

"Lucky guy," I reply, trying to mask the sorrow I feel inside. I guess Kristen didn't show her those photos.

She clears her throat. "How did you like the book?"

"It was good," I reply. "I've read it before, but it never gets old for me."

"I will have to admit that I've never really read it."

"Never? You're missing out."

"I'm more into romance books. There are not many here that I haven't read."

"Romance is definitely not my thing. Who is your favorite author?"

"Hmm, I've got a laundry list. None of which you would know if you don't read romance novels."

I shrug my shoulders. "You're not wrong."

She laughs. "How about this. I will read *The Odyssey* if you read a romance novel."

"You're on." What am I doing? I'm supposed to be letting her go.

She guides me back to the adult fiction section and pulls out a book. That thing must be six hundred pages long.

"You're not going to make this easy for me, are you?" I roll my eyes. "I suppose it's fair, considering you have twenty-four books to read."

"See, that's the spirit," she says as we walk back to the counter where Nancy is standing with her face all pinched up.

"I need you to do the sweep and do it good," Nancy bitches at Samia. "This morning, I found spaces and books out of place. I don't know what you and Kristen do with your time here. It's not like we are packed with customers!"

She's always so pissed.

"Let me know what you think." Samia smiles at me before disappearing into the confines of the building.

Nancy is shaking her head while she's scanning the book. She looks up at me. "You don't look like the type that reads romance."

"I am that type right now," I say. "Samia was immensely helpful. She really knows her stuff."

"Hmph. When she's not a sniveling mess, she's prancing around here with her head in the clouds." Nancy hands me the book. "Due back in two weeks."

I take the book and leave, all the while thinking about our first real conversation. Why is she still engaged? She couldn't have seen the pictures I sent Kristen, but she seems happy. Genuinely happy. I sigh because it's not me that made her that way.

6

Samia

"Why did I trust him again? That son of a bitch!" Here I am in the break room crying on Kristen's shoulders again.

"I didn't want to show these to you, but you needed to know the truth. I've had them for two weeks and went back and forth with myself about it. I knew showing you would crush you, but I can't stand by and watch him play you like this."

"I called him and told him about the pictures, and do you know he tried to lie about it? He told me he didn't know what I was talking about, Kristen's a hater, and those pictures were before we got back together. I would believe him if he didn't have on the exact same outfit as he did that night. And this Escalade." I pointed to the photo. "This was there, too. I'll bet anything it doesn't belong to anyone that works there. He's picking me up. I want to see his face when he looks at them! I want to punch his lights out!"

"I know you're upset, but he isn't worth catching a case. Just don't fall for any more of his lies. You deserve so much better than this."

Nancy comes around the corner into the sorting room. "That guy is out there waiting to speak to you. Take a break and get yourself together."

I walk around the corner and see Léoan standing there with the six-hundred-page novel I gave him. I rub my eyes and perk up the best I can, but he seems to know something is wrong with me. "Did you like it?"

"Are you okay?"

"Yeah," I lie.

"I can come back if you want."

"No. Let's go sit in the coffee shop." We walk around to the tiny shop snuggled in the front of the building and sit. It closes at five, so we have the whole area to ourselves.

"So, I read it and it's not bad," he says.

"I haven't had a chance to finish mine. I'm sorry." I look down and twist my ring. Cheap piece of tin! "Can I ask you something?"

He nods.

"Why are men such trash?"

"Because most of us think with our dicks."

I huff and look away, shaking my head. "I can read every romance novel in this library and dream up every true love scenario, and it still won't exist. Ever." I see him wince. "I'm sorry. I shouldn't be dumping all of this on you. I've just had a huge fight with my fiancé, and he has some explaining to do."

"Fights happen," he says.

"He has a problem keeping it in his pants."

"I can't imagine ever cheating on you."

"Have you ever cheated on anyone before?" I ask.

"To be honest, I did once," he confesses.

"Why did you do it?"

"Because I found the love of my life."

"So, the woman you cheated on didn't deserve respect enough from you to tell her you didn't love her?"

"The truth is that I thought I loved her. But it was lust disguised as love."

"Love, lust—the lines have become so blurred nowadays." I shake my head.

"I think the lines have always been blurred," he says.

"So, what happened to the side chick? Did you cheat on her, too?"

"No, she was killed, along with my unborn child. By the ex. That I cheated on."

"Oh, shit! I'm so sorry. I feel so foolish for what I just said."

"Although I can say that love was what brought us together, it was also love that tore us apart. I am completely at fault for all of it. If I had to do it again, I would do it all over but in a very different way." He looks intently at me. "As a single man, I would find you, and I would love you harder than I ever did before."

At that moment, familiarity hits me in a bout of déjà vu. I haven't had that for years. I enter a dream-like state, and this man looks to be farther away than he physically is. I can't get lost in this. I always do something out of the ordinary when I have déjà vu, so I stand up, still experiencing it, lean over, and I kiss him.

He stands up, grips the sides of my head, and kisses me back. His lips are so warm and soft—I melt into them...

"Samia, it's time for sweeps!"

I snap back to reality with Nancy standing there with her arms across her chest and tapping her aqua-colored kitten heels.

I touch my lips, staring at Léoan in disbelief from what I just did. What a way to escape that déjà vu! What was I thinking? Ugh, I'm not thinking, that's the problem! I race past him, not even attempting to hide my embarrassment.

With only thirty minutes left before closing, I sweep quickly because I just want to get the fuck out of here. I made a complete fool of myself. I get lost in the stacks as much as possible, then peer around a corner to see if Léoan is still there. He's at the counter with a couple of books. Okay, good. He's leaving. I sigh with relief and finish up my aisles. My lips tingle as I push the book holder to tighten the books. That was one hell of a kiss. He kissed me back, too. I'm lucky he didn't call SVU on me because I literally accosted him! Something triggered me into that déjà vu. When he was talking about his deceased girlfriend, it's like he was talking directly to me. I was completely there for it, too. I never noticed how hot he is before tonight. Olive skin, curly b ack hair, shapely pink lips. And those eyes! Blue like the ocean, and I'm not talking about the Atlantic. I'm talking about the beautiful clear blue oceans you only see on vacation brochures. I couldn't help myself. How could I? I have to clear my head of this. I have a bone to pick with Ace!

Kristen walks to me. "All clear on my side."

"Shit. I swept but didn't do my walkthrough!"

"I got you girl," she reassures me.

I thank her, grab my purse out of my locker, and go outside where Ace is waiting for me.

"Before you say anything, let me explain," Ace starts.

I pull my phone out and show him the pictures, aggressively sticking the phone in his face. "It better be a good explanation."

He looks at the pictures. "Aww, c'mon. That was way before we got back together."

"What about that outfit? That yellow shirt. That's the same shirt you had on the night you proposed to me!"

"Are you going to be okay?" Kristen asks as she and Nancy exit the darkened library.

I nod and fold my arms across my chest, not taking my gaze off Ace's cheating ass for a second. "I'll be fine."

Kristen gives Ace a drop dead look and then looks back to me. "Call me, okay?"

"Okay."

She and Nancy drive away, leaving me standing there alone with the liar. "I need you to be honest with me. One hundred percent honest for once in your damn life, Ace!"

"I told you I'm not with that hoe! What more do you want?"

"Fine, then explain that truck."

"What truck?" he asks, annoyance growing in his tone.

"That black Cadillac Escalade. I said I wanted one of those, and you said you would get me one when you hit it big. It's the same truck, Ace! I could hardly get out of the parking lot before that trollop showed up!"

"That probably belongs to someone who works there."

"At Applebee's? Someone that works at Applebee's has an $80,000 vehicle?"

"Yeah, sure. Why not? Look, just get in. Let's go!"

"Prove it!" I say.

"I told you that was long ago. How much more proof do you need?"

"Then you won't mind if we go to Applebee's and see if that truck's there? If it's not, we can ask the working employees if they have a coworker with that kind of ride."

"You're kidding me, right?"

"Nope" I shake my head. That is the only thing that can save your ass right now."

"I'm not doing all that! Get in the fucking car!"

"I'm not going anywhere with you until you promise we will go there."

"Okay, then walk your ass home! I don't have time for this psycho shit!" He gets in his hooptie and starts the engine. It sputters and dies before he fires it up again.

This motherfucker really out here trying to desert me ten miles from my home!

He rolls down his window. "I hope you're happy!"

I reach in and start scratching him and calling him everything but a child of God.

He rolls up the window, so I kick the driver door with my favorite ankle boots until he pulls off.

"Bastard!" I yell as that raggedy piece of junk he calls a car rattles away reaching its maximum speed of thirty-five miles an hour. "I hope you die!"

I sit on the curb and look around. Damn, him! Now how am I going to get home?

Léoan

THAT WAS...INTENSE, TO SAY THE LEAST. GEEZ, I DIDN'T think she had it in her. Wait, backtrack. Yes, she is very capable of whipping someone's ass when she's mad. As I watch her sitting there, I ponder if I should offer her a ride. Or would that seem too creepy? I mean, what am I supposed to say? How am I going to play this? I'm glad I didn't park in the actual parking lot, which I rarely do. Screw it. I have to get her home.

I pull into the library parking a little bit away from her and hop out. "Oh, man. Are you guys closed? I think I left the books on the counter." She looks up at me, clearly mad as hell. She's in a mood, so I have to tread lightly.

She nods at me while dialing a number on her phone. "C'mon Kristen, pick up."

I head to my car.

"Excuse me?" she calls after me, and I turn around. "I know this is weird, but do you think you can give me a ride home?"

I act like this doesn't elate me and that I have to think it over.

"I can give you gas money."

"Sure," I say, holding the passenger door open for her.

She starts toward the car. "Thanks. By the way, I have pepper spray and a Taser in my purse and I'm not afraid to use them."

"Okay." I close the door for her after she gets in.

The ride is quiet. She gives me directions on how to get to her place. I nod as if I don't already know.

"I should apologize to you for what happened earlier," she says. "I have no idea what came over me. It was like, at that moment, it felt like it was the right thing to do—the *only* thing to do. Even though right now I should feel extremely awkward, I really don't, and I don't know why that is."

"Well, I'm not complaining," I say.

She laughs and then looks out of the window. "I think I took things too far with Ace. I lost my temper. That doesn't happen often. I just have a really low tolerance for cheaters. I've been cheated on before so it kind of triggers me." She sighs. "What am I doing wrong?"

"Nothing," I say.

"There has to be something."

"Are you blaming yourself for your boyfriend's bad behavior?"

"No, but...why does it keep happening? I just don't get it. Maybe I attract losers, like myself."

Whoa, where did that come from! I pull to the side of the road, throw the car in park, then face her. "Do you attract losers? Yes. You know why you attract losers? It's not because you're a loser yourself, it's because you are everything they wish they *could* be. It's your energy. They want it. All of it. It makes up for what they're lacking. They want to feel good, so they drain you of *your* goodness."

"Energy? Who are you? You're speaking to my very soul right now!" She looks at me with wide eyes as I start driving again. "Turn left here," she orders me.

We turn into Avondale Arch Apartments, and with her guidance, I pull in front of her unit and park.

She sighs and looks at me. "I still have *The Odyssey*. Do you want to come up for a while and we study it?"

"I would love that.' *I really would love that!*

"Great," she says. "By the way, just a heads up, I have a loaded gun in my apartment so don't try anything."

"Are you sure you're not luring me in to kill *me*?" I ask.

She laughs and goes to grab her purse from the car floor. "Hey, your books are down here."

"Oh, silly me."

"Mhm. You can park in the guest spaces over there. I'm upstairs in unit 9B. I'll leave the door unlocked."

After parking, I walk through her apartment door and the first thing I notice is she's got books stacked everywhere. Books on the floor, on the couch and the kitchen bar. Two bookcases that she had run out of room were overstuffed and leaning in the corner. I've never seen anyone get that many books into a bookcase before. She's got skills. The washer and dryer to the left lead to a small open kitchen with a pass-through overlooking the living room.

She moves some books off the gray microfiber sofa and pats it. "I'll be right back."

While she's away, I take the opportunity to scan the bookshelves. Hmm, she's got a lot of romance novels, all right. She wasn't lying about that. I come to a section that's filled with books about reincarnation. What's this?

She comes back out donning a baggy sweater and sweatpants holding *The Odyssey* in her hand and notices I'm flipping through a book.

I look at her and squint. "You're not concealing your gun under those clothes, are you?"

"Ha! You won't have to worry as long as you keep your hands to yourself."

"Duly noted," I reply, putting that book back as I fish out another one with the title, *Have You Been Here Before?*

"Do you believe in reincarnation?" she asks.

"Very much so," I reply.

She sits on the couch, and I walk over and join her.

"You may be wondering what triggered me kissing you," she says. "I suffer from chronic déjà vu."

"Chronic déjà vu?"

She giggles. "Well, I haven't been diagnosed with it or anything and it's not as though it gets in the way of me doing daily tasks, but now it's mostly just annoying. I had an episode when we were talking. Usually, when that happens, I do something random in that moment. I feel like I'm changing my fate by not letting the déjà vu play through."

"Interesting," I say. "Feel free to do that again anytime."

She shakes her head and cracks open *The Odyssey*.

"How far did you get?" I ask.

"This page." She points to the first page.

"Really?"

"Yes, really. I was doubting your ability to get through a romance novel, and here I haven't even started the book I was supposed to read."

"Well, if it makes you feel any better, I skipped about three hundred pages of the book you gave me."

She gasps and puts her hand on her chest.

"At least I read half," I said. "Looks like you haven't even got past the title."

"You're right. And I wouldn't be holding it now either if you weren't here." She gets up and goes to the kitchen, returning with a bottle of wine in her hand. "Moscato?"

"Sure." It's not like it will affect me. Now, if I were humaning, that would be a different story altogether.

"I don't usually drink. Actually, this bottle has been sitting here for over a year. No better time than now to crack it open."

I want to say "sure you don't drink' but I don't. Considering how quickly she got tore up at Muse, she is definitely a lightweight.

She hands me a glass and sets the bottle down on the cherry wood coffee table in front of the couch. "Should we take turns reading chapters?"

"Now, I know you haven't even tried to read it," I say. "You mean book by book?"

"Look, I'm pretty knowledgeable when it comes to literature, but I've always avoided the *Iliad* and *The Odyssey*. These types of books just aren't my thing. The only history I'm interested in is World War II and Chinese Dynasties." She takes a sip of wine. "Plus, Nancy read them and said they suck."

Ouch. "You're going off of what someone else said?"

"Honestly, when I cracked open this book, the first words that came to mind were 'contrived' and 'tiresome.' The writer seems egocentric at best."

"You mean, Homer is egocentric and his writing is contrived and tiresome? How did you come to that conclusion without even reading it?"

"Cliff notes in college." She gives me an innocent look and takes another sip of Moscato.

"I think the characters are more egocentric than he is or was," I say. "It's quite possible you got a bad translation."

"Possibly." She downs the rest of her glass and fills it up again.

I start reading the first book and when I'm done, she's already gone through four glasses of wine. "Now, did that sound boring and contrived?"

"Kind of," she admits.

I hand her the book. "Your turn."

"Here goes nothing."

She starts off in a weird deep tone as if she's mimicking what I would have sounded like speaking the shit.

"He bound his sandals on to his comely feet, girded his sword about his shoulder, and left his room looking like an immortal gawwwddddd."

"Okay, now I see what you mean," I confess. "Hearing it read like that does sound a bit vain."

"I told you." She hums the words and takes another gulp of the Moscato.

"You're so cute when you're right," I say.

"You're always cute—" she clears her throat and catches her words.

No, baby. Tell me what's on your mind. It could have been the wine talking, but if she were drunk, how could she catch a slip-up?

She continues reading but this time in a regular tone. I sip on my wine as she reads. I'm playing like I'm listening very carefully to every word, every syllable. The way she pronounces the words rings with familiarity through my ears. I've missed this woman so much. I've missed her innocence, her intellect, and her feistiness. The words echo through me, and I go back to our first lives. The absolute best if you ask me. She's still the same in so many ways, even after all these years. She hasn't been tainted by so much of the nonsense that plagues this world, and she believes in second chances.

She hands the book to me, snapping me back to reality. "Your turn."

"Well done, Samia." I clear my throat.

She plays with the tip of one of her French braids.

She's playing with her hair. A good sign, no, it's a great sign! Everyone knows that's the universal sign that a woman is into you. I reach over and gently grab a braid myself. "Did it take long to do them?"

"This style only took about twenty minutes."

"It's pretty … you're pretty. Very pretty." I can't help myself.

We look at each other for a few seconds, embracing the silence between us with no words needing to be spoken. I lean in to kiss her, and she comes toward me with her eyes closed and I can't wait to touch those soft lips again. Our lips are just about to connect when her cellphone vibrates.

She stops and looks at it. A frown spreads across her face. "Will you excuse me a minute?" She walks in the other room.

I concentrate and listen to the conversation as best I can. It helps that she's buzzed because I don't know if she knows how loud she is.

"I don't know about that. I'm tired of this, Ace. I gotta go. I'll think about it."

She comes back and starts reading where she left off. This time she is reading the words, but it's like she's not here with me anymore. Her mind is somewhere else. Ace broke our connection just that quickly. I lean back on the couch as I realize I have no choice but to kill Ace and become him. That's the only way I can get her back. I've got to be a complete and utter dick to her. Even worse than Ace already is. He just can't seem to stay away from her, so I'll help him with that.

It's my turn again. I start reading where she left off. She's different now. Her entire demeanor has changed, and it's like she's not even listening. She curls up on the couch and rests her head in the corner. She's in some far-off place that I can't access. Still, I read on until she's snoring.

I close the book and set it on the coffee table next to a notebook. Curiosity gets the better of me, so I flip it open just to take a peek. A few old pages fall out of it. I look over at her then pick up a page and read a poem:

In Repose

My demons lie hiding
Invisible to the naked eye
They are quite charming
Yet sneaky
Hiding my true identity
They wait to strike viciously
Steady your steps
You either dance with them
Or leave the ball
I'm seemingly innocent
But you aren't lucky
You didn't hit the lottery
Although you may think so
I want you to sway with me
Feel the music from head to toe
Jump with me
Into my abyss of self-loathing
Cry with me—real tears
Understand why you are here
You can't save me
Only placate me
You will try
But
Like I said, My demons lie
In repose

Damn. My baby got more issues than Vogue. But I do too, so I can't really talk. I grab the pen that's lodged in the spirals and write my number down on the first page making sure to leave it open, with a little note:

HUMANING

You fell asleep. I was really hoping you would shoot me. Call me if you want to ...

7

Léoan

Ace is coming out of the music studio where he makes his shitty music when I approach him. What is that he's wearing? Baggy, tan Dickies with an oversized Oakland Raiders jersey. I didn't think it could get any worse than that getup he wore at Applebee's, but apparently it does. This guy is stuck in a 1990s gang movie. Are there even any gang members anymore? Oh, it seems I have left Samia to the wolves.

"Ace?" I say when we meet face to face.

He lowers his sunglasses and looks me up and down. He's wearing sunglasses at night. Wasn't there a song about that? The guy that sang that song was way cooler than this Tupac wannabe.

"Yeah?" he says in a baritone voice. His hair is slicked back with enough gel to satisfy a house full of Guidos for a year.

I'm going to enjoy doing this. He hurt Samia. That's a no, no. "I was referred to you by Georgie. He said you can do a cameo on my music video and rap part of my song."

He's still staring at me.

"I have money."

"Georgie didn't tell me anything like that. What's your name?"

"My name is Nick. and I go by Lil Nicky. Have you heard of me?" I play it cool.

"Yeah, I think I have," he lies.

I know he just wants the money, but he's playing like he's selective. "That's so dope! Maybe we can set up a t me to record together."

"Sounds good. Let me just call Georgie really quick—"

"I just got off the phone with him," I interrupt. "He's with his hoes. You know how he is about his hoes."

"That's funny because Georgie is married and I've never seen him cheat or his wife," Ace says.

So, he's not a cheater like you? Interesting. I figured birds of a feather flocked together. "Look, that's what he told me. Don't shoot the messenger."

He looks at his phone again. "How about you give me your number, and I will get back to you?"

"That sounds good. Let me get your number, too." I pull out my phone. "Ugh, it's dead. Do you have a pen and paper or anything I can write your number down with?"

He looks around. "Umm, I might in my car."

We head toward his car, and I finally get a good look at it. It's a 1986 purple BMW. He jams the key in the lock and opens the door, making a loud creaking sound, and I'm surprised Samia didn't put her foot through it the other night when they fought. What a pile of shit he drives.

He sits in the driver's seat and leans over to open the glove box. That's when I knock him out cold. His head lands on the steering wheel blasting the horn. I quickly push him over and slide in next to him. "Let's go for a ride."

I drive to a place called Lover's Cliff. It's dark, and there's only one other car parked there. I see people busy doing things this place is meant for.

Ace wakes up and looks at me, frightened. He looks around. "What is this?" He's scared shitless. Literally. I can smell him releasing his bowels into his pants. I thought he was such a gangster.

"I can't believe you shit your pants, man." I look at him with disgust.

"Wha ... what do you want from me?" he asks, still trembling and adding piss to the shit.

"I'm going to kill you." I like to get straight to the point.

"Kill me? Why? Somebody help, please!" He attempts to scream, but he's so scared he's squeaking like a mouse instead.

I chuckle and shake my head. "I really don't see what she sees in you."

"She?"

"Yes, she. Samia. You broke her heart, you know."

"I didn't mean to. It all just happened."

"Do you realize what she's going through right now?" I ask.

He shakes his head no.

"I didn't think so. Why would your selfish ass care, am I right? You only care about the new ass. I should have come sooner. I should have never left her vulnerable." I look out the windshield at the view. "She writes poems about you. I personally don't think you deserve that, but hey. I'm not her."

"Who are you?" he manages to ask.

I guess I can let him know. It's not like he will live to tell. "I am Homer. I am also Samia's soulmate. She thinks you are her soulmate, but she's wrong. I am. I will always be her soulmate no matter how many Aces come along. I wouldn't expect you to know me, though, because you're stuck in the 1990's." I roll down a window and let some of the odor out. "That's better." I look over to him. "Hey! Cheer up, man! You're about to hear the best story of your entire life."

He swallows a lump that's formed in his throat, then he nods.

"Samia and I were together in nine B.C. Although then, her name was Sera."

"Nine BC? What the fuck?" he says.

"Not everyone was happy about our relationship, especially not my ex-girlfriend Althea, the sexy, scintillating, psycho siren. Have you ever heard of Sirens? Of course, you haven't. Well, let me explain to you what a Siren is. Long story short, they are a cross between a woman and a bird. You do know what a bird is, don't you?"

He nods.

"They can also shift into many different forms. I fucked up and didn't protect myself and fell prey to one. Odysseus would have fucked up too had he not been tied to the mast of the ship. I thought my mind was too strong to ever give into a Siren. I was wrong. We passed by their land, by ship, Althea sang to me like no one else had, and for the very first time in my life, I smiled. I was enthralled. I was filled with lust. I ... lost myself. Althea was all I wanted—all I needed. Sirens were known for alluring and devouring men. Their lairs were said to have the bones of their lovers. Well, I took a chance on that. It was either be food or be fucked and luckily, she wanted to fuck. Every time we docked, she was there, at the shore. She had even shifted herself into a mermaid so that she could follow the ship around. She made the ocean her new home. For me. Always for me. You would think it was true love. Sure, she had her issues before and I'd heard bad things about Sirens, but I felt she was just misunderstood. And the sex!" I roll my eyes. "The sex was amazing. Have you ever had sex in the water?"

"No," he answers.

"You're not very talkative offline, are you? Your musician persona and what I'm seeing right now contradict each other."

He shakes his head back and forth.

"So, Althea and I were passionately in love, and I had to go on voyages often to document what would happen throughout the trips. Truth be told, I was surprised that Odysseus kept choosing me, since I had stopped recording, stopped writing stories, real and made up. I had no will to do it anymore. Althea took up most of my time, my mind, my very core. All I could think about was her and that ass. Woowee! She had me hook, line, and sinker. Pun intended." I smiled at Ace. "Do you know what a pun is?"

"No."

"I didn't think so. So … with every voyage I went on, I knew I was taking a risk. Boats back then weren't shit. They were extremely dangerous. Nothing like what we have now. Besides boats, all we had to get around were our feet and horses. We didn't have cars, buses, or planes like now."

Ace farts.

"Damn. We didn't have pollution like that, either. Crack the window."

Ace rolls down his window an inch.

"So, we would go on a voyage, and every moment I'd be itching to see Althea. One morning I was in the hold, umm...doing something. Okay, I was masturbating. I had to keep my shit together until I saw her again. That's when I heard a noise in the corner behind a stack of fruit baskets. I moved them and there was Sera, or as you know her now, Samia, and she was hiding. I could tell she was only a few years younger than me. She had shaved her head and dressed as a free man. We had many free men and slaves on the ship, but I knew right away she wasn't who she was pretending to be."

Ace grabs for the door handle, so I break his left arm.

"So rude," I say.

"Sorry," Ace whimpers.

"So, there Samia was, afraid and sweating profusely. Her beautiful brown skin glistened from head to toe. She sniffled, with her broad nose and with those big brown eyes she looked at me and pleaded with me not to tell on her. I asked her why she disguised herself and got on the ship, and she told me she ran away from her family and begged me not to tell anyone she had stowed away. She wasn't supposed to be there, but her father was very abusive to her. She told me he treated her more like a slave than a daughter, and that he had planned to marry her off to some ancient dude to bring their two families together. How could I ever turn her in?" I blink at Ace. "How could I?"

"I don't know," Ace manages to murmur.

"See? You get what I'm saying." I pat him on the shoulder.

Ace groans.

"Soon, I was sneaking food and finding hiding places for her so the other men on the ship wouldn't find her. *Particularly Odysseus.* He would have kept her for his own, I have no doubt about that. In that time, we got to know each other, I mean really got to know each other. There was no sex, no lust, just real deep conversation. She not only had a beautiful outside, but she was beautiful inside as well. So, I fell for her. Hard. You understand that, don't you?"

Ace nods.

"And I started writing again. I had ideas again, I made up stories again, I was me again. I didn't even realize how lost I'd been. I recorded a lot during that trip, and when we docked, I sneaked Samia off the boat and subsequently sneaked out of everyone else's lives, Althea included, or so I thought. Who was Althea, Ace?"

"Um, she was, um, a Siren or something."

"Just checking to see if you're listening," I say. "Let me tell you about the city of Nikaia. It was just off the water, and that's where we settled down. As a cautionary measure, I told Sera to stay away from the water and the shore. Not just because of Althea, but because her father may have sent ships looking for her. We found a place together and lived— I mean, *really* lived. I can't remember a time when I was happier. Sera not only put a smile on my face—she kept it there. We made love, we didn't just fuck. And we talked, really talked and we wrote, sang, and danced." I look up at the sky. "I loved her, and she loved me." I look over at Ace. "And now, she loves you. Imagine that."

He swallows nervously.

"I had gotten a job teaching, and I was at work when Sera went down to the water. We were expecting our first child then. She was ... called. I know she was. I specifically told her not to go near the water, and it was dangerous. Of course, as soon as she got there, Althea dragged her in and drowned her. As if that wasn't enough, Althea also cursed Sera to live over and over again. When I went to find her, I found her dead. I'll never get that picture out of my mind. Her, lying there with her big stomach, my child inside of her perished along with her. Althea came to the shore, and you know what she said to me, Ace?"

"No."

"Of course, you don't know," I say. "Because you weren't there. Althea smirked and told me, 'She will never be yours. She belongs to the universe now. Nobody crosses me and gets away with it! As such, it is your turn.' That's when she cursed me. To live out the rest of my life as a ghost shark. The ugliest fucking shark that existed. She wanted to make sure nothing or nobody liked me. Not even other sharks. Daily I begged for some ship to come and harpoon my ass. I couldn't stand it!"

"But ... you're here. You're not a shark."

"Very good, Einstein. What gave it away?" He's sitting there still stiff as a board with his hands folded in his lap like a scared little boy. So pathetic. This is the heartbreaker.

"I'm not a typical vampire, Ace."

Ace slams his body into his door. "You're a ... a vampire?"

"Yes, sort of," I say, I'm unique. Some would say what I have is a gift, but to me, it really isn't. I've never been able to sit at the vampire table. I was never accepted by them. I am too different. I can do something they can, but I also can do things that they can't. Because of this, they both hate and envy me. I'm not one of them. I am an 'other.' A mutt, so to speak. They can't do the very thing that I am going to do to you. I am going to become you."

Ace shrinks into his seat more. "What do you mean?"

"I'm going to become you. The entire package, the whole "Ace" enchilada. That's one of those things regular vampires can't do. Your body will be mine."

His eyes bulge like a fish deprived of oxygen.

"The bottom line is cheating doesn't pay, but to be completely honest, this isn't all your fault. I mean, technically it's not. It's mine. Had I not been so enthralled with Althea and left her alone in the first place, Sera and I could have lived a normal life and died as husband and wife like normal people do." I look over at Ace and study him. "Because of me, she's fallen victim to bad decisions and very bad taste at that."

"I don't understand why you have to kill me," Ace says. "I won't tell anyone what happened here. On God, I won't. And I'll never talk to Samia again. My word is bond."

He finally pleads for his life.

"Yeah, I can't do that," I say. "As long as you exist, she will never see my love clearly. Besides ..." I nudge his broken arm. "I have plans for your body."

He starts panicking again. "Please, I'll do anything. I mean anything." Ace nervously licks his lips and looks down at my crotch.

"Whoa, slow down there. Is this what you're doing to break into the music business? Judging by your music and bad YouTube videos, your head game is trash. I wouldn't take you up on that offer even if I were interested. I'm appalled you would think so low of me. After all this time, we've been hanging out here. I'm spilling my guts and all you can think about is sucking my dick? I realize we are at Lovers Cliff, but geez, man, control yourself."

"No ... I ..."

"I'm getting tired of you and the way you smell." I give him a dirty look and look past him as the couple next to us have finished with their business and start to back out.

Suddenly, Ace bolts out his door and runs toward their car, flailing one hand in the air and yelling for help.

The car stops, and the woman gets out. "Oh my God!" the woman shouts. "Are you okay? What happened to you?"

Dammit, Ace! I pull the keys out of the ignition and exit the vehicle to go after him. I get there and he's pointing at me, telling the woman and her man that I'm going to kill him.

I raise both my hands in the air. "I'm sorry. It's my drug addicted brother."

The guy is out of the car now, not knowing what the hell is going on.

"Well, maybe we should take him to the hospital!" The woman looks at her man.

"Yeah, he looks to be in pretty bad shape," the man says.

I look at the guy. "I'm taking care of it. I mean, look at him. He's obviously got mental issues. He's coming off drugs and I refuse to give him anymore. He's soiled himself he's feening so bad. Go on ahead and go home. I've got this."

"I think he's got this," the man says to her.

"Why would he be running away from him then?" the woman asks.

I look at her. "You should listen to your boyfriend. Both of you should leave here, right now. I promise I will get him the help he needs."

She nods, and they get in the car and take off leaving me standing there alone with the little shit that tried to escape.

And now he's crying.

I sigh loudly as I approach him. "You're not going to make this easy, are you? I was going to show you some mercy but this stunt you pulled has made me decide otherwise. You're a shittier friend than you are a boyfriend." I race toward him and punch him in the throat before he has time react. He falls on his knees holding his neck and coughing. I circle him like a predator. "How did you meet Samia? Don't worry, I'll wait until you can talk."

After another moment of his dramatic retching, he answers me. "I met her at a club. We had a one-night stand, and she found me online and asked me to go out with her. I just wanted to hit it and quit it, but she got totally obsessed with me. We would date and break up, and she would come begging me back. She's a psycho just like you."

"You calling my baby a psycho?" I kick him in his mouth, denting his fake gold grille. He falls back, gasping, and spitting blood.

"Just kill me!" he says, finally talking like he has some balls, which by the way, I crush to put him back in his place. Now he's holding his nut sack, or what used to be his nut sack. "I thought you needed my body!" he yells.

"I need your DNA. It doesn't matter what shape your body is in." I shake my head at him. So pathetic. "You know what? You listened to my story, so I'll cut you some slack. I'll let you run, give you a good head start. Don't worry, I won't cheat. I think you've earned at least that."

"Thank you, thank you so much!" He crawls then lurches to his feet and starts to run away the best he can

I lean against his pile of tin and count to one-hundred and he's still in sight. I roll my eyes. He's not going to be any kind of a challenge. He's gimping and looking at me and when he turns back around, I am in front of him.

Shocked, he holds his hands out. "Wait, please!"

"Time's up!" I grab him by his jersey and drag him back to the edge of the cliff.

"No, no!" he screams as I toss him over the edge.

Ace hits every sharp rock, edge, and corner of that cliff, and I jump down seconds after him, using his body for a cushion. He hits the bottom, and his limbs look like a puppet's limbs, stretched every which way but correct. He blinks and looks at me, paralyzed from the fall. I kneel over him and drain him, and as I do, I feel I am draining every ounce of love he got from Samia that he didn't deserve. Every time he had sex with her, every night he fell asleep next to her. It's all mine now!

I convulse as the transformation takes place, and I turn into the very thing I couldn't get rid of, but I turn into someone that I know for sure Samia loves, regardless of how big a piece of shit he is.

I remove his soiled clothing and put them on myself, minus the underwear then take what I hope is his house key off the keyring and throw the rest of them on top of his corpse. Then I walk back to town.

As Ace.

The things I do for love.

8

Samia

On a day off, I'm lounging on the couch reading *The Odyssey* when there's a knock at my door. I look out of the peephole and see that it's Ace, so I quickly open the door. He looks terrible. And smells terrible to boot. "What happened to you?" I grab his hand and bring him in.

"I had an accident." He stares at me, standing there like a helpless kid.

"Ugh." I plug my nose from the putrid smell he's emitting. "I can tell. You need to get in the shower. I still have some clothes you left here."

I leave him standing in the middle of the living room and start the shower. Whatever happened to him, it must have been bad. He literally shit himself. I've never seen him like this before. I go back to the living room, and he's just standing there waiting, not saying a thing. I grab his hand and lead him to the bathroom.

"I got you a fresh towel and a robe hanging on the rack for when you get out." I start to walk out when he grabs my hand.

"Stay," he says, as he gets undressed and gets in the shower.

What the fuck is wrong with him? What happened to him? He's not talking and I'm worried to death right now. "Are you going to tell me what happened to you?" I stand on the other side of the shower curtain. I wait a few seconds, and then peek around the shower curtain. He's standing there, letting the water cascade down his body.

He reaches for the body wash, picks it up, and then hands it to me. "Wash me."

I grab the loofah sponge and squeeze soap on top of it. Then I scrub his back, down to his hips, buttocks, and legs. Then he turns around and I repeat the same in the front while he gives me another odd stare.

"Why do you love me?" he asks.

"What?"

"Why do you love me?" he asks again.

"I just do."

"But I cheat on you, I'm an asshole and a liar, and I shit on myself. But here you are bathing me like I'm a child. Is there anything I can do to make you stop loving me?"

"Why are you acting so weird? Whatever, I'm not doing this with you right now." I throw the loofa at him and leave the bathroom.

A few minutes later, I hear the water stop and soon he comes to the living room butt naked and soaking wet. "Let's fuck."

"Excuse me?" I say.

"It's not like we haven't done it before." He starts jerking his dick right in front of me.

"What' the hell is wrong with you? The way you're acting, there is no way I'm having sex with you! You're disgusting me right now!"

"I'll just get it from someone else then."

"Ace, what the fuck!" I say. "What happened to you? What is all this?"

"Make me a sandwich," he orders like he's the boss of me.

"What? No!"

"If you love me, you'll make me a sandwich."

"Ugh ... I ... Ace, I'm not making you a sandwich."

"No sex, no sandwich. What good are you? I'm your man. Feed me, fuck me, give me what I want!"

"Ace, stop this!"

He narrows his eyes at me, and I stare back at him. "You know I don't love you, right?"

"That's not what you were saying the last time we talked," I say.

"I tell you what you want to hear because I know no matter what I do, you will never leave me."

Smug bastard! I open my front door. "You need to go!"

He goes to the bathroom and puts on his clothes then comes back. "I'll be back tomorrow after I see my other girlfriend. She's got no gag reflex. She's real talented."

Did he just ... "Get out, Ace! Now!" I start to tear up. "I don't' have to put up with this!"

"But you have been." He shrugs. "There is literally nothing I can do to make you leave me. You're the perfect girlfriend. Perfect and dumb."

I go to my bedroom, get my Glock 17 out of my underwear drawer, go into the living room, and hold the tip up to his fat head. "I. Said. Get. The Fuck. Out."

His eyes widen. "You're going to shoot me? How will you live without me?"

I clench my teeth and pull the safety.

He starts backing out until he's standing outside.

I keep the gun on him while I retrieve the plastic grocery bag, I put his shitty clothes in and launch it at him, hitting him in the head. Then I start to slam the door in his face when he stops me.

"Wait, please!" he begs. "Just one more thing."

I squint and wait for what he's going to say next. "No begging or 'I'm sorry' will work anymore with me. You crossed the line! What can you possibly say next?"

He lifts his right leg and releases a loud, obnoxious fart. "That."
I slam the door in his face.

9

Léoan

It had to be done. I had to make it so the last time she saw him, he was being unforgivably fucked up. I know she's taken him back for worse, but she almost shot me, so that's a good sign that she's sick of Ace's shit. I've got about two days until someone finds his body at the bottom of that cliff, so I head to his house to enact the rest of my plan.

When I arrive at the address on his license and use the key to unlock the door, as soon as I walk in, I see a very large woman planted on the couch. Her thighs are ten times the size of her calves. I can tell she doesn't get off the couch much.

"Richard, I've been calling you all night! Where's the food?"

"Food?"

"Yes, the food you left here to get hours ago. Me and your brothers are starving!"

Just then twin boys no older than six run up to me. "I want McDonald's, I want McDonald's!" They push each other and fight over who's going to get the nonexistent food first.

"I forgot," I say.

"Again? I swear I can't depend on you for nothing! You're just like your daddy!" She rolls off the couch and waddles off like a penguin to somewhere in the back of the house.

"Don't worry, Ricky. Mommy's just in a bad mood today. Can we get the McDonald's now?" One of them looks up at me, innocent and wide-eyed.

"Yeah, sure," I lie. "I just have to do something really quick. You guys didn't mess up my room, did you?"

One of them laughs, but the other one just stares at me.

"Hmm, I'll bet you did. Come with me and prove you didn't."

I follow them down to the basement that is apparently Ace's room. He's got music equipment all over the place and a computer wedged in the corner next to a mattress on the floor. I get on the PC and see that it needs a password. Figures.

"Hey, what's my password?" I squint at the two little boys. "I know you know it."

One of them shakes his head, smiles and puts his hands over his face.

"I'll give you extra fries if you tell me."

"Don't tell him!" the other twin says, the one that likes to stare.

The nice one motions for me to lean in closer and whispers "cripwalker94."

Oh, my fucking gosh. I roll my eyes and enter the password. Then I turn to them. "Go upstairs, I hear Mommy calling you." The nice one leaves, but the evil one stays. Of course.

"You're not Rick," he says with his arms folded across his chest.

"What are you talking about?" I ask, shocked.

"You're not my brother."

Is this kid serious? "Of course, I'm your brother. Run along."

"You're not my brother!" he yells.

I look at the stairs and make sure no one is coming down. "You must not want McDonald's. Don't yell anymore."

"I don't care! You're not Rick! You're a monster!"

"Monsters eat people. Did I eat you?"

"No."

"Okay then go back upstairs."

"Not all monsters eat people. Just because you didn't eat me doesn't mean you're not a monster."

I grind my teeth with annoyance. "Well, I'm the eating kind of monster, and I'm going to devour you if you don't leave me alone."

"I'm not scared," he says. "I'm not afraid of monsters!"

I contemplate kicking him up the stairs and making a field goal through the basement door, but I take a softer approach. "What do I have to do to make you be quiet and go away?"

He goes over to an old oak dresser, opens the top drawer, and pulls out a wad of cash. Then, he looks at me with his narrowed eyes. "I want this. If you don't give it to me, I'm gonna tell my mommy you're not Rick."

"She's not going to believe you," I say.

"Yes, she will. My mommy believes everything I say."

What an evil little shit.

"Take it," I say.

"And don't forget the McDonald's," he reminds me

"How am I going to buy McDonald's if you have all the money?" I ask.

He starts counting the bills in front of me and gives me a crisp twenty. "Don't give Dante extra fries. He's greedy. He always gets extra and he eats up everybody else's, too."

I roll my eyes. Dante's greedy, but shaking me down for all my money isn't? Although it's technically not my money. Still, this kid is a piece of work. "Okay." I point him to the stairs, again. I wait until I hear the door close before I start typing.

Dear anyone that cares,

I am typing this letter to my loved ones. I'm tired of being such a useless piece of filth. I hate myself so much. I'm ugly with a small penis and have bad taste in clothes. Because of these factors, I have decided to end my life. Please don't be mad. I'm a loser and I will never make it in the music industry. The world will be a better place without me. I gave all of my money to my little brother. Not Dante, the mean one.

Farewell, cruel world. -Ace

That oughta do it. I get up and go back upstairs when Dante greets me at the top.

"Mommy's crying again."

"Because I didn't get the McDonald's? I ask.

"Yeah. She said you're a deadbeat, just like daddy."

I massage my temples, head for the front door, and get out of there as quick as I can. Wow! I guess you really don't know how a person lives until you are in their shoes. I almost feel bad for Ace's little brothers. Not enough to regret killing him though.

I walk about a block and dial an Uber to take me to the nearest McDonald's. When we get there, I damn near order the whole menu. I tip the Uber driver an extra twenty bucks to take the food back to the house, then I walk home from there. The deed is done. This has been one hell of a day.

JUST AS I SUSPECTED, ACE'S BODY IS FOUND FAIRLY quickly. I've still got about a week and a half before he wears off me, so my only choice is to lay low for the time being.

Unfortunately, I will have to be away from Samia, but there is no other alternative. I can't exactly pop up anywhere as Ace.

I log onto Facebook and see that Ace's mom has used his Facebook page to tell all his friends that he committed suicide. There are several comments giving condolences. Do I feel bad yet? Nah. With my burner account, I go to the post and comment on the status:

Ebony Smith Oh, wow! I can't believe he's gone. He had so much potential. Woooooowww!

I'm such a dick.

I scroll through the comments when I see one made by Samia.

Mia Greysen   OMG! ☹ ☹ ☹

She's better off without him.

Suddenly there is a knock at the door. Who could this be? I peek out the corner of the blinds and see it's Samia! How does she know where I live?

"Léoan? Are you there?" She knocks again.

My phone goes off in my pocket. Busted. It's her. Shit, shit, shit! Umm ... okay. I clear my throat and answer. "Hello?" My voice is barely above a whisper. If anybody would recognize Ace's voice, it would be Samia.

'Hey, where are you? I'm at your apartment. I hope you don't mind I got your address out of the system. I really need to talk to you."

"I've been really sick." I cough. "I'm losing my voice, so I can't talk long."

"Oh. I'm sorry to hear that," she says. "Is there anything I can do? Want me to pick you up some soup or something?"

"No, the doctors told me I'm really contagious. I'm surprised I'm not getting you sick over the phone."

She giggles. "You're sick but still have a sense of humor. I like that."

I smile against the receiver. I like *you*.

"Well then, call me when you can talk, I guess."

"I promise," I say.

"Bye."

I stay on the phone until she hangs up. I don't want to let her go. I want to be with her right now. She's here, mere feet away from me and I can't look at her face to face. I'm stuck in Ace's body, and I'm already sick of it.

10

Léoan

⁓⁓⁓⁓⁓⁓⁓

"Hey, you!" Samia greets me as I walk through the library doors. "Feeling better?"

"Much," I reply.

"That reminds me. I finished *The Odyssey*."

"You did? Hmm, if I'm not mistaken, you called it contrived and—"

"Tiresome, I know, I know," she interrupts. "But I ended up enjoying it."

"Did you enjoy it enough to read the first book?" I ask.

"Okay, I didn't enjoy it that much." She laughs.

"I guess one out of two ain't bad."

"It's time for my break. You think we can talk for a little bit?"

Of course, you can talk to me until my ears bleed! "Sure," I reply coolly.

"Same place?"

We have a place now. I like that. "Sure."

"Let me tell Nancy I'm going on break and I'll meet you there."

I nod and go to the coffee shop. She joins me there about five minutes later and sits next to me.

"I came over last week because I needed someone to talk to. Ace killed himself."

"What? That's crazy."

"Yeah, it was such a surprise. The whole time we dated, he never expressed any kind of suicidal thoughts or anything. He was too narcissistic and self-centered to do such a thing, but he did act strange the last time we talked. He came to my apartment and said some awful things. I had to pull my gun on him to get him to leave."

"NO! Sounds like the guy was unhinged."

"I guess so, because he offed himself that night. The police say they found him at the bottom of Lover's Cliff. They say he jumped. I guess he wrote a suicide letter at his house before he did it."

"I'm sorry to hear that." *Not!* "I know how much you cared for him."

"You know, the strange thing is the way he acted that night lessened the blow in a sense. I'm sad, but I'm not as sad as I should be and I don't know if I should feel guilty about that or not." She shrugs her shoulders.

"You had no control over what he did. I didn't really know him, but judging by the way he treated you, I don't think he was a good person."

"I'm not going to lie, there were some good things about him, but—"

Suddenly she goes silent and leans forward, her face becoming closer to mine. She grabs my shirt collar and plants one on me. I can get used to this. I close my eyes and savor it. This right here is what keeps me coming back. Everything melts away in these moments. When I am with her, I feel complete.

"Léoan?" She says my name and breaks me out of my daze. Her lips have already parted from mine.

"Another déjà vu?" I ask.

"She nods, leans over, and kisses me again. This time even longer.

"Another one? That was fast."

"Nope, I just wanted to kiss you that time," she says. "I gotta get back to work."

"What are your plans for this weekend?" I strike while the iron is hot. "I would love to take you out."

"I have to wash my hair tomorrow, and I have to visit my dad on Sunday."

Annnnd, strike! The old, I have to wash my hair excuse.

"Before you think I'm using my hair as an excuse, I'm not. I really have to do my hair tomorrow. With my type of hair, it's an all-day thing."

"Maybe next week …"

"You know what? Come by tomorrow. I'll start on my hair early, that way we can go out."

"You just want a free meal, don't you?" I joke with her.

She gasps, "You found me out!"

"You can use me all you want." I say.

"Ha! Careful what you ask for." She gets up. "Tomorrow around noon-ish?"

"Is noon-ish a word?"

"It is now," she replies.

"Well, who am I to argue with a librarian?"

She chuckles and goes back to work.

Tomorrow it is, Samia.

11

Léoan

I get to Samia's five minutes early and knock on the door. She opens it, and as I walk in, I notice she's got the same style. "Did you rebraid it?"

She gives me this guilty look like a kid caught with his hand in a cookie jar.

"I ... sorta didn't start yet."

"Mhmm."

"I'm sorry. I got lazy and started watching YouTube videos." She sits on the couch, and I sit next to her.

"Well, it looks fine to me." I'm not lying. Her hair could look like George Jefferson's, and I would still think she's beautiful.

She starts unbraiding one of them and sighs.

"Need help?" I offer.

"Would you?" she asks. "Do you know what to do?"

"It's a braid. It can't be that hard."

"I've been meaning to ask you what you do for a living. I always see you in the library."

"Oh, I...uh. I am a physical therapist. I rehabilitate bodies."

"Oh, wow, that's so awesome. Do you know how to give massages?"

"Yes, I can." I'm not lying. I've lived long enough to perfect them!

"I might be needing one after all this," she laughs.

Say no more, baby. Say no more.

She points to the braid she's assigned for me. I unbraid it while she does the other one. Her hair texture is thick and silky, just like it was when she was Sera. After we are done, she shakes her head until it's puffy like a lion's mane. She looks so cute.

"Okay, now I have to wash it. Do you want to watch TV? I should be out in about thirty minutes."

I point at the bookcase. "Nope, I'll just find something there."

"Okay." She nods, and soon I hear the bathroom door close.

I grab a book off the shelf. *To Kill a Mockingbird.* It's been a while since I read this one. Wonderful classic. I crack the first page open when I hear her calling me. When I get to the bathroom, I open the door and peek around. She's sitting in her bathtub wearing just a bra and panties, with water raining down on her from the shower spout.

She looks at me. "Do you think you can help me some more?"

"I ... umm, yes?"

"Was that an answer or a question?"

"Definitely an answer," I reply. "Let me just ..." I fumble with my clothes and remove my shirt then my pants until I'm just wearing boxers.

"I knew you weren't a tighty whitey guy." A bit of a smile crosses her face for the first time since I got here.

"Sit behind me."

I get in, wrapping my legs around her body so that my crotch meets her lower back. I try to concentrate and hope nothing "pops" up but seeing her like this is going to be hard not to. I scoot back a little, making room between us, just in case, while she hands me a black large-tooth comb.

"We do it in sections. You do the back two and I'll do the front two." She dips her head in the shower and gets her hair nice and saturated then she parts it in four sections and lathers them up with something that smells like coconut as she explains to me how to hold and comb each section. I do just that, trying to ignore the water cascading down her shoulders, back, then her hips. Annnnd ... I'm hard now. Really, really hard.

I detangle my other assigned piece then hand her the comb over her shoulder. She grabs it from me but holds on to my hand for a long time. When she lets go, I run my hands down her shoulders and start giving her that massage I promised her.

Her skin is so soft—*like touching smooth silk.* I inhale and exhale trying to keep my composure as she moans when I'm kneading. I work from her shoulder blades to the balls of her back, then down to her hips and her black panties. Rubbing back upward, I lean down then kiss the nape of her neck and watch as little goosebumps appear one by one.

"How do you know that's my spot?"

"Lucky guess," I reply, as I kiss it more, and this time, I pull the bra straps down.

She leans back into me when I unbutton the clasps and using both of my hands, I massage her breasts.

She pulls the bra completely off and throws it outside of the tub then she throws her hands back and around my head, giving me full access.

I use both my hands and cup her breasts, caressing her rigid nipples while licking and nibbling her neck. My blood is boiling. I'm hungry for her. I want to consume her but not like the others. I want to feel every inch of her body against mine.

She turns around, straddles me, puts her hands around my shoulder, and kisses me.

A shiver runs down my spine as I wrap my arms around her and squeeze down to her soft ass where I rip those little panties off and discard them next to the bra. Then I kiss her eagerly, my tongue memorizing the texture and curves of her lips, getting to know how this Sera tastes and feels, and it is heaven. Pure, unadulterated heaven.

She sees my hard, throbbing cock with the tip peeking out the top of my boxers, and she looks surprised. A pleasant surprise, I'm sure. She pulls them down slightly and grinds on me as steam builds in the room. I want her so bad. It's been so long. I take my cock and rub her wet spot in circles.

Then she gets up and out of the shower holding my hand to guide me to her bedroom.

She fiddles through her nightstand and pulls out a rubber and hands it to me. Her body is like a work of art So wonderfully and beautifully made. I put the condom on the tip, and roll it down as we kiss more, our tongues swirling in and out, back and forth. Sloppy tongue kisses and I'm loving every minute of this.

I tip her on her back and slowly enter her. Her warmth encompasses me inch by inch until I'm all the way in and she arches her back, gasping with satisfaction.

"Take it all, baby," I whisper. "It's all yours."

Her nails dig into my back muscles as I move inside of her in a circular motion, getting her wetter and wetter, preparing her for when I increase my pace. The bed squeaks, playing a song of two lovers reuniting in the dead of night. Music to my ears. I am lost in this moment. She stares at me as I stroke, then she takes her thumb and rubs my bottom lip before biting it, then licking it.

I want to come so damn bad, but I hold off, giving her the pleasure I know she needs and deserves.

We both moan in each other's mouth, kissing through the moans, and I can't hold back anymore so I pull out of her then go down, licking her beautiful folds and parting them to get to the lush, pink spot. This pussy is good. Amazing! Exemplary! I tongue her from the bottom and back to her clit, licking it and working it in circles.

She grabs a tuft of my hair and holds my head as her breathing gets heavier.

"Come," I command. "Come for me, baby."

She spreads her legs wider and starts convulsing, releasing into my mouth what feels like centuries, decades, and years of frustration, coating my tongue with her warm juices. I lap it up like a dehydrated man finding an oasis in the Sahara Desert.

While she's still coming, I enter her again and slide back and forth while rubbing her clit. She's close again. I can feel her muscles tightening around me.

"I'm coming again! Oh God, I'm coming!"

This time I come with her, our juices mixing in a perfect symphony of sweat, love, lust, and desire.

We both come down, but I stay lying on her, kissing her neck, chest, arms, and stomach, leaving no spot undiscovered.

She gives me a strange look, as if she's looking inside of me. She turns her head and sighs as I lay down next to her. "That was perfect."

"You're perfect," I whisper.

She sniffles and wipes away a tear. "It's like you knew every inch of my body by heart."

I do know. I know her, and I also know why she's crying.

I embrace her, enjoying the silence until we fall asleep.

Later, Samia wakes terrified and breathing hard, jumping straight up out of her sleep.

I quickly hold on to her. "What is it?"

"A bad dream."

I hear her heart beating rapidly.

"I haven't had that dream in a long time," she confesses before drifting back to sleep.

I lie awake for the rest of the night, just in case she wakes up again and needs me. I will be here.

SAMIA WAKES ME AGAIN, ONLY THIS TIME SHE'S happily jumping up and down on the bed. I can't believe I fell asleep again. I had planned to stay up all night. I suppose I drifted off because I am so damn comfortable around her.

"Get up, sleepyhead," she says, her hair whipping around.

"Your hair," I say.

"Yes." She flips it to one side. "I flat ironed it because we have somewhere to go today."

"And where would that be?" I ask.

"We are going to visit my dad. Remember I told you the other day?"

"I get to meet the parents already?"

"Yes, you do," she replies with a smile. "So, get your booty up!" She throws my clothes at me and stops jumping. After landing on her knees, she leans over and gives me a kiss. "Wow, you just woke up and your breath doesn't smell weird. Inhumanly possible." She sticks her tongue out at me, and I catch it with my teeth, bringing her in for another, longer kiss. I love this playful side of her.

"Do we have to leave this room?" I ask, seriously wanting to stay here all day and explore every inch of her body again.

"Yes." She pulls away then throws a pillow at me. "I made breakfast already. We have to leave soon."

"I need to stop by my place to get something to wear. I want to impress my future in-laws."

She uses her fingers to comb through the side of her hair, looking away and blushing while leaving the room. I knew I loved her, but I *really* love *this* her. How she is now is so different, yet the same. Loving the same person, but different. Crazy, kinda

12

Léoan

❧

"Bald Head Island is an Island off the coast of North Carolina. I grew up there with my father and Meg."

"Meg?"

"Short for Megaera. She's technically my adoptive mother, but I don't' claim her since she's always been such a bitch to me."

We park across the street from the Bald Head Is and terminal then catch the ferry. We ride for about thirty minutes. The whole time Samia sits on my lap and snuggles her head in my chest, making sure not to look over the edge of the boat.

We arrive and disembark. Waiting for us is a white-haired man with leathery bronzed skin standing next to a golf cart. He looks like he is in his early sixties, and he's wearing gray slacks with a white polo shirt.

"Daddy!" Samia runs to him and hugs him.

He hugs her back tightly, "Hey, pumpkin! So good to see you." He looks over to me. "Who's he?"

"This is Léoan. Léoan, this is my father, Finch Greysen."

"Nice to meet you, Finch." I shake his calloused hand.

"You got a good grip on you, son," Finch says. "Nice to meet you, too. Samia's never brought any of her boyfriend's here. You must be special," he laughs.

Okay, so he's a funny guy, I guess…

Finch helps Samia into the front seat of the golf cart with him while I sit on the back and quickly realize how uncomfortable it is. We drive over a sandy driveway, hitting every rock and bump on the ground.

"There are no cars allowed here on Bald Head Island," Finch explains. "We either get around by foot, by bicycle, or by golf cart. It's a nice escape from city living."

Soon we pull up to a huge wooden stilted house just off the ocean shore. We ascend the steps and go inside. The living room extends into a huge kitchen the size of mine and Samia's apartments put together. A sliding glass door leads out to a balcony with two tables covered with umbrellas and a kick-ass view of the water. Off to the right of the tables are stairs that lead directly down to the sand.

We round the corner to the kitchen where a woman is hovering over a white and gray marbled kitchen island. "I didn't realize you were bringing company, Samia."

This must be Meg. That greeting alone shows me what Samia was talking about. No "How are you daughter" or a hug or an "I miss you?" I'm already seeing why Samia hates her.

Samia rolls her eyes then grabs my hand. We walk to where Meg is cutting fresh fruit on a wooden cutting board. A black dog barks and runs to meet us. Samia leans down and pets him, ruffling his big ears. "Hey, Bo!"

I freeze as Bo licks Samia then immediately comes to me, barking and jumping on me.

"Get down!" Samia orders, then baby talks him. "Silly dog. Be easy on company, you silly dog! Yes, you're a silly dog. Who's a silly dog?" She looks at me. "I think he likes you!" Samia pets him once more as he stares at me, barking and whining.

"Léoan, this is Meg, my wife, and Samia's mother," Finch says.

Meg uses her forearm to brush away dark caramel-colored bangs and looks at me with dull gray eyes. She gives me a half smile with full lips stained with ruby red lipstick. Well, it's more like a smirk. "I didn't know Samia was dating anyone."

"Well, neither did I," Finch says.

"Hmph, can't say I'm surprised she hasn't told us." Meg looks over at Samia. "Mia likes to keep things from her parents. Important things."

"Ah, stop," Finch says.

Samia rolls her eyes and looks at Finch. "What are we doing today?"

"I was thinking about some fishin'," he replies.

"Ugh. You know I hate fishing."

"Yes, I know, but maybe Léoan here wouldn't mind coming with me."

"I'm not much of a fisher," I say.

"Well, I'm a good teacher," he laughs again. "Besides, Bo hasn't been to the water in a while. He loves fishin'. Otterhounds love to swim."

"They have webbed feet, so the water is second nature to them," Samia explains.

I look at Bo, and he stares back at me, tilting his head. He *is* kind of cute. I'm not a huge fan of dogs, but I think I can deal with this guy.

"We'll be back," Samia tells Finch and Meg and leads me up upstairs. "I'm going to show Léoan around."

We walk through the house. There are about four bedrooms, Finch and Meg's being the biggest one, including a whole room for Bo."

"Your dog has his own room?"

"He doesn't really go in it, only when he gets in trouble and he wants to hide, which is actually pretty funny seeing as he hates his room."

"Bo is a spoiled brat." Meg chimes in from behind us. "Samia, your father wants to talk to you in the kitchen."

Samia grabs my hand.

"Alone." A fake smile crosses Meg's face.

"I'll be back." Samia squeezes my hand before leaving to join Finch in the kitchen.

I give her the "Don't leave me" side-eye which she doesn't see, but Meg does.

"That's cute," she says, but I have a feeling she doesn't mean it. "How long have you two been together?"

"A long time." It's technically true. Samia just didn't know we were together yet.

"How old are you?" she asks.

I clear my throat. "I'm thirty-three."

She plays with her necklace, then rubs the blue teardrop-shaped pendant between two fingers, looking me up and down. "You're not her type. Did you know her ex-boyfriend?"

"I knew of him, but I didn't know him," I reply.

"Do you know he just died recently?"

"Yes, I do."

"Do you really think it's a good idea to date Samia at a time like this? She's mourning and isn't thinking straight."

"I understand your concern for your daughter, but Samia and Ace haven't been together for a while and if Samia feels she wants to be alone, all she has to do is tell me."

She goes from rubbing the pendant to caressing the top of her chest, moving over her lowcut blouse, stopping at the breast area.

I think she's trying to seduce me. I watch her, not being able to tear my eyes away from her. She takes a step toward me, then puts a hand on my chest. Her hand drifts down, stopping at my crotch, where she rubs it. I get hard and I feel guilty as hell about it.

I'm a whore.

Meg pulls away just as Samia comes around the corner. She stops and holds my hand and looks back and forth at me and Meg. "What I miss?"

"Nothing, dear. Just getting to know the new boyfriend."

"He's great, isn't he?" Samia says, a smirk crossing her face.

"He's definitely something," Meg replies, sashaying back to her husband where she belongs.

"Come on." Samia leads me to a room that's nothing like the rest of the crisp, bright house. This room looks a little like a basement. The window is covered by a black sheet, and the walls are plastered with Metallica, Slayer, System of a Down, and The White Stripes posters.

"This is my room. My parents have kept it the same since high school."

"I thought you were going to show me the house."

She smirks. "I'm showing you the only room that counts."

I study the walls. "I knew you were a metal head."

"Well, technically The White Stripes aren't a metal band, but I love their music even though they are not a band anymore. Classic stuff. And I like alternative as well."

"How did Ace feel about that?" I ask, bringing him up for the first time in days. "I mean, he was all about rap and hip hop."

"You knew his stuff?"

Shit

"Well," she continues, "he mainly ignored the fact that we had different taste in music. He always played his music or some other rapper. Sometimes he would play old school R&B. He did hate me wearing black all the time, so I implemented more colors in my wardrobe."

"You changed a part of who you are for him."

"Pretty much," she says.

Now that we are someplace where I can ask the obvious question that's been itching me since I first saw her parents, I ask. "Umm, so, Samia?"

"Yes?"

"Your parents are white."

"Mhm." She nods. "They adopted me when I was about one. So, they say, but of course, I don't remember anything because I was so young. To tell you the truth, the earliest memory I have was when I was six years old. It's as if it took me six years to start living."

"Maybe you blocked the earlier years out. I'm no therapist, but usually that happens when you've experienced some kind of trauma."

"Yes, I know, Dr. Léoan," she teases me.

I sit on her bed and sigh with satisfaction as I sink into it. It's as if it's swallowing me whole in its plushy goodness. She closes her door, stands in front of me, pushes me back, and then straddles me.

"We should have sex," she whispers.

"Are you serious? Your parents are downstairs."

"So?" she says, leaning over and nibbling my neck.

And I'm hard already. "Yes, I want to have sex, but I'm a somewhat respectable guy."

She unbuttons my jeans then pulls the zipper down and realizes I'm not wearing any underwear. "Easy access," she smirks.

I put my hand over hers. "Samia, stop. We can't do this now."

Samia ignores me, removes my hand, and starts pulling my pants down. She is making this really hard! Pun intended! I pull them back up then she pulls them back down giggling until I'm running around the small room trying to get away until she corners me. Where is SVU when you need them? This house is one big sexual assault, but Samia gets a pass.

Fuck it. I tried. "Oh, geez, you got me cornered," I grab her face and bring it to mine, planting a kiss on her lips, then sucking her bottom lip while she runs her hands over my black and cyan gridded long-sleeved shirt, fiercely unbuttoning it.

"You've got an incredible body," she says after disposing the shirt. "Just like a Greek God or something."

Hmm, I am Greek and I knew gods. Close enough.

I pick her up, guiding her legs around my waist while I shimmy out of my jeans and lower her to the bed. She reaches over the side of the bed and gets a condom out of her purse, which I put on then slide in with one swift motion, watching her moan and tilt her head back. God, she feels good. I bury my head into the nape of her neck and lick and suck there, being careful not to bite her. She grabs me around the back and guides her hands up and down my rippled muscles, digging her nails deeper the farther I go. I savor each and every moan that falls from her plump lips. She's so perfect. Everything about her is perfect. I pause to look into her eyes. She looks back at me, and I see that spark! Yes, that spark that tells me that she feels the same about me as I do about her. Familiar spark.

"You're so amazing," she says to me through labored breaths.

I'm amazing? No, she's amazing! I'm falling deeper in love with her by the day, hour, minute, and second. Something I planned from the start, but I didn't know it would be this intense.

She takes my head in her hands and runs her fingers through my hair, and after bringing my face to hers she kisses me, using her tongue like a dart and she's hitting the mark. Oh, is she hitting the mark.

I pull her dress up and over her head as she helps me then throw it on the floor. This is becoming our own little routine. I leave her mouth and move down to her round breasts and lick circles around the large dark brown areolas, then take each erect nipple into my mouth, one at a time, lavishing them like a starving person lavishes a hot meal. And I am starving for her. I have been starving for her for centuries. Here I am again, inside of her, holding her, kissing her, tasting her and I can't seem to get enough.

I increase my speed, moving rapidly in, then out, then back in circular motions. I am filling her up completely, and I don't want out. Not now, not ever. I keep the movement going until she arches her back in release. I pull out and spread her legs wider, putting them over my shoulders, then I go downtown, licking, slurping everything, mixing it with my saliva until it is spotless. Again, I have to taste every bit of her like a greedy man at a buffet.

She wraps her legs around my neck and tightens them, running her fingers through my black locks, matching the rhythm of my tongue with her hips. I grab her soft, round ass and squeeze as I dart my tongue in deeper, then go back to licking her clit until she releases again and I take it all. Again.

"I love you," I tell her when I finally come up for air.

She looks at me, surprised with a little bit of confusion mixed in. She reaches down for my face then brings it up to hers and I follow. She looks into my eyes and says, "I love you, too. I didn't know it was possible to fall in love this soon, but I do love you. I love you like crazy. It's weird, but I am one hundred percent certain of it."

Yes!

We are both spent and we lay side by side on her bed, me breathing heavily and looking at the posters on her walls.

"That was by far the best sex I've ever had," she says, kissing my chest then laying her head on it.

"Better than yesterday?"

"Yes."

"I got plenty more where that came from." I wink at her while running my fingers through her hair. The texture is so much different than it usually is. Not like the usual.

"I straightened it because I didn't want to hear Meg saying anything. She's always got something negative to say about my appearance."

"Yeah, but what grows out of your scalp is natural. How can she be mad about that?"

"I don't know. I think she hates everything about me. She made that clear a long time ago. Nothing is ever good enough for her."

I grip her chin so that she's looking at me. "You're more than good enough. In fact, I think you're too good for a lot of people."

She smiles then kisses me softly.

"Speaking of too good, why did you stay with Ace? I am genuinely curious. Did he even bother to take the time to really get to know you? How did you get wrapped up with someone like that?"

'I met him online. One day he messaged me and said he liked a poem I wrote. He asked me if I wrote song lyrics as well because he was a musician. I told him no, but we talked about other things. I didn't think much of him at first, because he wasn't my type at all, but every day he kept messaging. I don't think there was a day that went by that he didn't send me a good morning text. He grew on me. After a few weeks, he asked me out to dinner, and it went from there."

I knew he was lying about how they met. "So, he was nice at first or…"

"I mean, he was okay. He was cool. I did see some narcissistic tendencies he had, but I overlooked them."

"Why?" I ask, genuinely puzzled.

She looks at me, closes her eyes, and sighs. "I didn't stay with Ace because he was a good man. I stayed with him because he made the déjà vu go away. I didn't have it when

I was with him. So many years I've struggled with it. Day in and day out. I know you read that poem from my notebook. I wrote that poem when I was six. My dad read it and freaked out and took me to a therapist. That's when I told them about the déjà vu and the dreams. I've been on depression meds, anxiety meds, had several CAT scans ... all of it and nothing helped. I just had to deal with the realization that I might be crazy. So, some might say that Ace used me, but in actuality, I was using him too. That's why I kept forgiving him for doing the things he did."

"Did you ever think you were having the déjà vu because you are supposed to remember something?"

"No." She shakes her head and turns away. I don't want to remember. I don't want to remember because it's awful. I know it is. I can't even have peace in my sleep. The dreams are always the same. I'm in a body of water and I'm drowning and I am with someone who drowns, too, but I can't see who that person is. All I know is, I feel so much loss when I wake up. It's painful."

It sure was.

"Ace turned that all off, and I didn't care if it was selfish of me. I ... just ...I didn't want to know the when, where, or why. I still don't. I want to live in the here and now. Finally, for the first time in my life, my mind was silent and my ignorance was bliss, but now the dreams are coming back slowly and I'm having déjà vu again along with déjà rêvé which means "already dreamed." But the déjà rêvé started with you that day at the library."

I don't know what to say to her as I realize just how much I may have fucked up. Ace brought her peace, but now Ace is dead thanks to yours truly. I know why she's having these episodes, but I can't tell her yet. She won't believe me.

Do I get down on my knees and beg her to remember? Beg her to fight her fears and come to love? There is no other being on this earth who can love her the way I do. I've searched for her high and low for centuries, and time and time again I've endured the heartache of losing her. It hasn't been easy for me, either. But how can I expect her to suffer as I do? It hasn't been enough for me only to know that she exists. I want to be a part of that existence. She is the whole reason I keep going. I power through it all and go forward because I know she will be the prize awarded me once I do make it through. But for how long? Each time I feel it's going to be different, and we will be able to live happily ever after. Together until the end. We were never afforded that luxury our first time around or any subsequent time after that. I want that happy ending, but will it be to the detriment of her mental stability? I love her so much, but it kills me to see her hurting—

to see her scared—and I can't blame her for not wanting to recall pain.

There's a knock at the door and Finch is on the other side. "Léoan, are you ready to go fishing?"

I whisper to her, "Did I really tell him I would go fishing with him?"

"No, but you didn't say you wouldn't," she reminds me.

"Ugh." I get up, put on my clothes, and stop at the door. "You owe me."

She throws a pillow at me, which misses and hits the door while I'm shutting it.

On my way to go fishing with Finch.

13

Léoan

I meet Finch outside at the golf cart and hope he doesn't make a pass at me on our excursion. He's got fishing poles, a pail of bait, a tackle box, a tripod, a drink cooler, and some beach chairs all stuffed in the back seat with a rope wrapped around to keep everything in place. I absolutely hate fishing. In a way, I feel like I'm killing family, so I avoid it altogether. But for Samia, I will play the dutiful boyfriend and humor her dad. He seems really cool anyway. Him and Meg are opposites.

We park where the sand is shallow, then I grab the beach chairs, the cooler, tackle box, and tripod. He grabs the fishing poles and the bait bucket and we find a spot.

I set the stuff down and we unpack it. After unfolding a green and white vinyl beach chair, I realize I haven't seen one of these things since the 1980s. Finch hands me a fishing rod and points to the bait. I take a deep breath and get a night crawler out and press it onto the hook. Here goes nothing. I roll up my pants leg and trudge about ten feet into the water until it hits my calves, then I cast out the line.

Finch walks up and joins me after setting his stuff up. He stays at a distance but not too far that we can't talk because apparently, that's what he wants to do.

"Dusk should be hitting us pretty soon," he says. "That's one of the best times to fish from the shore. The water is nice and calm. It's the perfect time to come out."

"I have to admit that I'm not a fan of fishing." No sense in lying.

"I kind of figured you weren't," he says, "but I'm glad you obliged an old man."

Finch gets a tug on his line, so he pulls it up and backward then reels in the catch. "That's the quickest I ever hooked one. You must be good luck." He laughs, taking the hook out of the fish's mouth while it frantically flip flops.

"I guess it's fish for dinner," I say, a little grossed out.

"Ah, hell," he says as he throws the catch back in the water. "Meg would never let me cook 'em. Catch and release is all I do."

Interesting. Maybe Meg has a heart after all. We're silent for a few moments as the waves becoming more turbulent by the minute. I feel the water rising higher on my calves and feel seaweed wrap around my ankle. I have a love, hate relationship with the sea ever since I was doomed to live in it so long ago. I'm glad that all that is behind me.

"I never liked Ace," Finch says unexpectedly. "I never met him in person, but Samia told me everything that happened between them. I told her to leave him from the moment he first hurt her, but it was something about him that she couldn't let go of. It's frustrating to see your daughter hurting and there's nothing you can do about it. She's grown and makes her own decisions now so all I can do is be there for her if those decisions go wrong."

"You won't' have to worry about Ace anymore," I say, quickly realizing how cold I sound.

"And I am grateful for that. The funny thing is that Meg was a big supporter of their relationship, even though she knew about everything. Seems like it didn't matter what he did, Meg was always under the impression that they should stay together."

"I noticed the interaction between her and Samia," I say. "It was kind of awkward, to be honest."

"Meg and Samia have never gotten along. It's ironic because Meg was the one who wanted to adopt her in the first place. Once we brought Samia home, I fell in love with her, but Meg acted like she didn't care for her anymore. She checked out when it came to the motherly things she should have done. Supporting Samia financially is all Meg really did. That's why I stepped in and did all the rest. I went to Samia's school plays, doctor visits, you name it. If Samia needed me, I was there."

I look out into the water. Doesn't make sense that Meg would want Samia then basically discard her when she got there. Then again, she just felt me up with her husband mere feet away, so I'm not going to put it past her. Nothing about Meg makes sense.

"Samia doesn't come out here to the water often," Finch says. "She's feared it since she was a little girl. She almost drowned when she was six. It was right out here, as a matter of fact. Samia was playing in the sand, and the tide came in way farther than it usually did and swept her out. Good thing Ajax was with her when it happened."

"Ajax?"

"Ajax was our old otterhound that passed away. He went on in the water and dragged her out. Boy, I miss that dog. He was like a guardian angel. A few days after he died, that's when Bo arrived. Otterhound, just like Ajax. He was right down here when I found him, in this exact spot. His coat was ragged and he was extremely thin and malnourished, so I figured he was a stray or got lost. I took him in, and when no one claimed him, I made him ours."

"That's wild," I say.

"Yep. After a while, I was able to teach Samia how to swim, but she wouldn't stay in the water for long before she had bad anxiety. I was told she would grow out of it but looks like she never will."

I get a tug on my line and ignore it, but Finch doesn't.

"Reel it in!" he shouts.

I reluctantly lift and pull, hoping the fish will somehow get itself off the line. I realize that this is no ordinary fish because of the sheer weight of it. Curiosity gets the best of me, so I play the struggling fisherman and fight with it, pulling up then backward and I'm starting to get frustrated because whatever is on the end of that line is jerking the line every which way but where I need it to. I am going to pull this fish out of the water! Time to end this show. I pull once, using my real strength, and the line breaks as a baby shark sails in across the wet sand.

'Look at that! You got you a shark!" Finch laughs. "That's crazy because the only bait you were using was nightcrawlers. It's their time to be close to the shore though."

I feel like shit. I walk over to it, flipping and flopping, digging its fins deeper into the sand. I pick it up and try to remove the hook that I lodged in its mouth. It's a baby tiger shark that's about one and a half feet in length. It looks at me, and I see pleading in its eyes. I stick my hand further down its mouth and find the hook, take it out, and throw it back in the water.

"Now that right there deserves a beer!" Finch opens the cooler and hands me a Bud Light. We sit in our uncomfortable chairs, and he props the poles up in the tripods. We sit for a few minutes taking in the view.

"I'm in love with your daughter."

Finch takes a big swig of his beer, finishing it in one gulp, then crushes the can and sets it in the sand beside his chair. "I know you do. I can tell. Just promise you won't hurt her like Ace did. Don't hurt her at all if you can help it. I know she can be a little confusing at times, but she's an amazing girl and she's a blessing to anyone's life she comes into."

And he's right. She is all those things, and now I know why he wanted to go fishing so badly. This was our father, boyfriend "heart to heart," so to speak. It feels really cool. I've never had one of these. It's clear he loves Samia almost as much as I do, and I'm glad she has him in her life.

When the sun totally goes down, we gather up the stuff, put it on the golf cart, and head back to the house. When we get to the porch, Meg greets us at the door and looks us up and down. "Shake yourself out there and leave your shoes. You're not going to track sand into my home."

"Yes, dear," Finch says.

I look at Finch and wonder how he does it. Meg is so miserable and has a horribly negative vibe emanating from her. Not to mention she flirts with her daughter's boyfriend. When we walk in, I notice Samia is still in her room, probably hiding from Meg. I wish she had a real mother to look up to.

I go to her room to find Bo sleeping at the foot of the bed. Holding a pen and paper in her hand, Samia looks up at me. "How did it go?"

"It was good. I think your dad and I bonded."

"He likes you. I can tell."

"He seems like a pretty fun-loving guy who likes everyone."

"Meh, he is, somewhat. I think he just tries to balance out Meg's crazy."

"That makes sense."

"Putting up with her for a few hours is a small price to pay to see my dad." She shrugs. "What is your family like? Are your parents still alive?"

"My parents are long dead," I reply. "I never really knew my dad, but my mom was a quiet, gentle woman. She loved to write. That's where I get that from."

"I didn't' know you wrote. That's impressive. What do you write?"

"Just stories about adventures, voyages and such." I'm not lying. Technically ...

"Do you have anything published? What's your pen name?"

"Nope, just do it for fun, between times with clients." And that right there *is* a lie.

"Samia!" Meg calls from downstairs.

"Oh, speak of the devil." Samia rolls her eyes and gets off the bed then bends down and rubs the cover. "Keep it warm for me." She winks at me then leaves the room.

14

Samia

What does meg want now? I find her in the kitchen, hovering over the island, her favorite place.

"Have a seat, Samia." I see she's already started drinking and I immediately know where this is going. "What's new?" She asks me as if she gives a shit.

"Nothing much," I reply.

"How did you meet the new guy?"

"His name is Léoan and he's just a good friend," I say.

"Mhm," she says drinking her wine and side-eyeing me. "That's not what he told me. He said you guys have been dating for a long time. Ace is still fresh in the grave and you're gallivanting around with a new man? Honey, that's not a good look." She downs the wine from an oversized glass then fills it up again. "What did I tell you about keeping up appearances?"

"Keeping up appearances? For what and to whom?"

"What I'm trying to say is, maybe you should take some time to yourself instead of injecting a new person into your life. You know how you get when you're ... stressed."

"Don't worry, I know what I'm doing," I say. "This right here is exactly why I didn't want to come talk to you. You're always busting me up and judging everything that I do."

"Here you go, playing the victim card again. I'm only looking out for your best interests. You've always had a problem keeping a boyfriend. There's always something one way or another. Consider taking a break and finding yourself first so you don't subject this poor man to your drama. Like you did Ace."

"Are you kidding me? Ace killed himself, for fuck's sake! I had nothing to do with that."

"I wouldn't be so sure about that." She tilts her head. "I would probably kill myself, too, if I was with you."

My eyes widen, and a cold shiver runs down my spine. She's always been a bitch, but she has never been this bad. Who is this woman?

"Meg, that's enough," Finch says, walking into the kitchen. "Why can't we enjoy being together as a family?"

"Finch, she needs to hear this," Meg says. "You've always catered to her every whim. She needs to know that the world doesn't revolve around her."

"I never said that it does!" I yell.

Meg takes another sip of her wine. "I'm just trying to help."

Léoan walks in, rubs my shoulders, and leans down and whispers, "Let's go."

"Excuse me, but I'm talking to my daughter!" Meg spits at him.

"That's what you call this? Talking? You've done nothing but put her down since the minute she got here."

"Hey!" Meg yells, her face twisted up. "When I need advice on how to handle my family, I will come to you! You come to my house and tell me what to do? I don't think so! You don't know me, you don't know Finch, and you certainly don't know Samia."

Finch gets in front of Meg and tries to calm her down. He attempts to take the wine glass, but she jerks it away from him and spills it all over me. I stand up, in shock, then run out the front door and down the steps with Bo hot on my heels. After I get a good distance, I start walking to the ferry. I don't care how dark it is, I have to get the fuck out of here. She completely embarrassed me in front of Léoan. Now, he's probably thinking I'm a basket case or something. I know one thing—he knows that my family sucks. Well, *half* of my family, anyway.

As I'm walking, Bo walks with me. "No, Bo. Go home." Of course, he doesn't listen. Soon I hear footsteps behind me.

"Samia," Léoan calls me. I stop in my tracks. He walks up behind me and hugs me. "It's okay."

"Out of all the mothers I could have had, I got wicked Witch of the West."

He turns me around and hugs me. We stand there embracing each other until my dad drives up.

"Samia?" My dad is sad. I can hear it in his voice, and I think he's crying, although it's too dark to tell. He gets out and hugs me. I don't blame him for Meg. I can't. I know he loves me, but he also loves her for some unknown reason. I've always wished he would divorce her. Just leave her to wallow in her miserableness, but it's as if she has a spell on him. It's always been that way, so I take the good, which is my dad, with the bad, which is Meg.

He kisses my forehead. "Honey, I'm so sorry. I don't know what came over her. I've never seen her act like that before. C'mon, get in the cart. I'll take you guys to the ferry."

When I get home, I immediately go to the bathroom, shut the door, and turn on the shower. I get undressed and sit in the bathtub, letting the water run over my freshly laid hair, turning it back to its kinky texture.

Léoan comes in after me, gets undressed, and sits behind me. This time he caresses my hair and he whispers. "You don't need to change for anyone. You are perfect the way you are. If others can't see that, then it's their loss."

"I'm never going back there." I break down and cry. I'm so glad I held it together in front of Meg, but now I'm free to feel. I'm free to express whatever emotion is going through my head right now. I'm with a wonderful man who I love, and I have no doubt loves me. So, I cry a mix of happiness and sadness, and Léoan holds me through it all.

I WAKE UP IN THE MIDDLE OF THE NIGHT FROM another nightmare. Léoan is there to hold me. I do feel bad. Seems like he has to sleep with one eye open. "Thank you for being here for me."

"I love you, I love being here for you, but Samia, there will be times when I can't be here. Just know that I'm thinking of you in those times."

"I will and maybe they will get better. The déjà vu has. Maybe I just need to get it out of my system?"

"The déjà vu is better, so, all those random kisses?"

"I just like kissing you."

"Ooh, I like the sound of that. You should kiss me right now."

"Only if you promise me one thing," I say.

"And that is?"

"Promise to tell me if this becomes too much for you. Don't just ghost me."

"I'll never ghost you. If I get sick of you, I'll tell you to your face."

I hit him a few times with my pillow.

"What I do?" he asks, playing innocent.

15

Léoan

Samia and I have been going strong for a good while now, but it is time for me to become human again. I had to make something up. Something believable. I hate that I lied to her, but I had no choice. I decided to tell her that I needed to go on a business trip, traveling with sports teams and giving some of the athletes' physical therapy.

It was hard for me to leave her, knowing how bad her dreams have gotten, but it had to be done. I will not only scare the living shit out of her if I don't feed, but I will also have to divulge my secret in a way that I don't want or intend to. So, here I am again driving down No Man's Land, looking for my next body. Who will I be for the next couple of weeks?

If I'm going to be human, I need to make sure I will be as comfortable as possible. Don't want another Montrell incident.

I'm walking down the street when a man asks me for money. He can't be more than 30 years old and most likely, he's asking for money to buy drugs. Hmm, tan skin, shaggy golden-brown hair, about 5'7, 160-ish pounds, scraggly beard ... He will do fine, and he looks to be healthy enough. He's actually a really good-looking guy. Not the norm for No Man's Land. What could possibly go wrong?

I lure him to my car where I drive a few miles away and then drain him easily enough. I'm coming back from dumping his body when I look in the rearview mirror and run my fingers through the thick, nappy beard. This shit is itchy! If there's such a thing as crabs in one's beard, then this guy had it. I'm going to have to fix this. A little beard oil and a trim ... maybe.

I love beards. I used to have one way back in the day when I was my human self. It's clear to me the guy didn't know the importance of well-maintained facial hair. I fit in perfectly with the millennial douche bags, and I love that being human still gives me the opportunity to keep an eye on Samia, although now that Ace is out of the picture, there shouldn't be anything to worry about. I do, however, hate her mother. Samia doesn't need that kind of negativity in her life.

I scratch the beard and begin to formulate a plan to kill Meg, but if I do kill her, I will be hurting Samia's dad, which in turn hurts Samia. The very daughter Meg can't stand is the one that's saving her life right now.

Suddenly, I see police lights behind me and a siren blaring. I immediately pull over and lean back in my seat. The cop comes and taps on the window with a flashlight which he then shines in my face.

I hate the police.

I roll the window down and smile at the officer. "Hey, officer, how are you tonight?"

"Step out of the car, please."

"Is there something I did?" I ask.

He puffs out his chest. "Step out of the goddamn car! Now!"

I comply, open the door, and step out. He throws me to the ground like an angry bear swatting a honeycomb dangling from a tree. Then he jumps on my back and jerks my hands behind my back. He then pulls out his gun and steadily points it to my head. "Don't you move a muscle! I will light your ass up! Try me, mother fucker!"

His partner comes charging in like they're arresting a black man selling loose cigarettes.

They are so lucky I'm humaning.

"You have the right to remain silent," the second officer says.

"Wait." I try to look back. "What the hell did I do?"

He shoves my head into the asphalt. "We saw you get in that guy's car back there. Now, he's gone and you're driving. Where's the body?"

Shit. There is a body, but it's not the one you're looking for. "I don't know what you're talking about!" I shout.

"We know your type. Typical entitled little fiend. What happened? Did he not offer you enough money for sucking his dick, so you killed him and stole his car?"

"He gave it to me," I say. "I dropped him off."

"Like I'm gonna believe a dope fiend from No Man's Land. You're going to jail! Save the bullshit for the judge!"

He and his partner lift me to my feet, then walk me to the cruiser.

"You have the right to remain silent and to refuse to answer questions," the second cop says, "Anything you say may be used against you in a court of law. You have the right to consult an attorney before speaking to the police and to have an attorney present during questioning now or in the future. If you cannot afford an attorney, one will be appointed for you before any questioning if you wish. If you decide to answer questions now without an attorney present, you will still have the right to stop answering at any time until you talk to an attorney."

"There's been a lot of people coming up missing from there lately," the first cop says. "At the very least, you're going down for car theft!"

After roughing me up more than I need to be, they throw me in the back of the police cruiser and take me straight to jail. I do not pass go, I do not collect two-hundred dollars, but I *do* collect 50,000 volts of electricity ripping through my body and possibly a concussion. When we get to the county jail, they immediately release me to booking where I am asked my name and other various questions I don't know the answer to, so I make the shit up as I go.

I get my mugshot taken, I'm fingerprinted, then I'm in a holding cell with half a dozen other men where concrete floors, walls, and steel benches run around the room attached to the concrete walls. I sit on the hard bench contemplating what the fuck I'm going to do to get out of this one. This is bad. Very bad. How long will I be here and where will I be when I change back? I won't be able to see Samia. I know I can't see her as myself since I'm supposed to be out of town working, but I could at least go to the library to keep an eye out for her. Anything could happen while I'm gone. The officers weren't lying. I am a fiend. Samia is my dope. I need to see her.

"Hey, bro." A man big enough to dent the steel bench comes over and sits next to me. I hear the creak and wait for it to give way, but it doesn't. This guy has gotta weigh at least four-hundred pounds, but he's got the height to offset it.

Before he starts, I ask him. "Let me guess. You're going to be a cliché and ask me what I'm in for? Then you're going to tell me you're the baddest motherfucker in here and to not try shit? This is the part where I tell you I'm in here for murder. So, don't fuck with me!"

The guy laughs, and his eyes become even more narrow. "You got it all figured out, huh?"

"You're supposed to call me a tough guy," I say and he laughs more.

"I was going to ask you how long you've been growing your beard. I can't seem to get past five o'clock shadow. What's your secret?"

"The blood of my enemies. Lots and lots of it."

"You're hilarious. I'm Kailao, by the way."

"I'm ... just a guy with a beard."

"Okay, Just a Guy. What are you here for? I'm in for a DWI myself."

"I'm really not sure why I'm here." Which is true. "I just know those cops didn't like me very much. How long do they keep us here?"

"Eh, we will probably go before the judge in the morning. Then we can post bail or get out on O.R. or we will go to gen pop. Or, if you're really lucky, they'll take you to a psyche ward and give you the good stuff."

And that's my way out of this mess. Thank you, Kailao. In order to do this, I have to pull this off flawlessly. I scan the room and my eyes land on a guy lying on a bench at the opposite end of the room. He's sleeping like a baby. But not for long. I walk over to him and bite his ear like a rabid dog biting a chew toy wrapped in red meat.

Mike Tyson has nothing on me.

He bolts up right away. "What the hell is going on!" Blood starts dripping down his ear profusely.

"Oh, shit! What did you do?" Kailao can't believe what he just witnessed.

The guy sees the blood, starts screaming, and all hell breaks loose in the cell.

Five officers rush in and take me down, tasing me again as I yell, "I am Sir Braveheart! I am Sir Braveheart!"

Take me down to Paradise City.

16
Samia

"What you thinking about?" Kristen asks me as she walks up behind me daydreaming at the front counter.

"Nothing," I say, but I'm really thinking about Léoan and wish he would call me. He did, however, tell me that he wouldn't really be able to contact me, but he would if he could. Traveling with sports teams, they are always on the go. I should have expected this silence, but I would still like to get a text to let me know that he is okay.

"Have you heard from Léoan?" she asks, worried that I let another Ace in my life, but we just don't know it yet.

"He's working," I respond. "He will be back in a couple of weeks."

"Ladies, I need you to at least try to look busy," Nancy tells us.

I am so sick and tired of her bitching and moaning every day I'm here working. It's like she got worse since Léoan and I started dating. Miserable old bitch.

I go to the back room and check the return bins for holds. That's when she comes back to join me.

"You've been awfully chipper lately." Nancy smirks with deep red matte lips.

"Mhm." I shake my head, trying to ignore her.

"It's that guy, isn't it? Tall, dark, handsome and a little creepy?"

I stop searching and look at her. "Yes, it is him, minus the creepy part."

"I guess you didn't notice him here for weeks before you guys started talking. He would sit and stare at you for hours. If that's not creepy, I don't know what is. Have you done a background check on him or anything?"

I squint. "Look, I appreciate your concern, but I know what I'm doing, and I know him very well."

"Well, as long as you know what you're doing. I'm just saying it was as if he appeared one day out of thin air, but maybe it's just me."

"Where else do people appear out of if you've never seen them before?" I retort.

"You've only been dating him for a month or two and you think you know everything about him? Little girl, you've got so much to learn." She shakes her head.

I laugh nervously because I'm trying to keep my composure, so I don't knock her ass out. "Yes, I do, and who better to teach me than you, Nancy. Since you're married and all—Oh, wait. *He's* married, not *you*."

She huffs, frustrated and looking at me crazy surprised that I finally had the balls to call her out on her shit. We stare at each other in a silent showdown when Kristen walks up. "Nancy, there's a lady out front that wants to talk to a supervisor about a book that's missing. The system says we have it, but it's not on the shelf and she won't take no for an answer."

Thank you, Kristen.

Nancy clicks away to go deal with the unhappy customer.

"I heard her in here giving you the third degree," Kristen says. "Nice clapback, though!"

"Girl, what the hell is her problem? She's taken an unusual interest in my dating life ever since Ace. Like, I don't know her like that. It's none of her business."

"I think she likes Léoan, to be honest. Every time he's around, she can't take her bulging eyes off of him. I can't say I blame her for finding him attractive because, girl, he puts the F, the I, the N, and the E in 'fine.' Plus, he adores you. She's just mad because she's a single side chick."

"Right? She's the epitome of a bitter mistress." We giggle when Nancy rounds the corner back into the sorting room.

"There's nobody out there," Nancy says. "Did she leave?"

"Oh, I guess she did," Kristen says as I hold back laughter.

"Get ready for sweeps, you two," Nancy orders. She goes into her office and slams the door.

"I swear if I didn't need this job," I say. "I would cuss her out and keep it moving! Everything was fine until she got hired. She doesn't do anything but sit on her ass in her office all day unless Léoan's here or she's getting in my business. Truth be told, I should be the head librarian right now, but I swear she got that job on her knees for the chief librarian."

"Yup," Kristen says. "He's never going to leave his wife for her."

"Who knows? The way he salivates over her when he's here is just ... yuck! He's totally infatuated, and I cannot understand who would be infatuated with that old, rickety ass wench."

"Let's be honest. The chief is no prize either. I mean, he looks like he's in his third trimester."

"With twins!" I say, and we both laugh.

"I'm just glad to see you're happy again, and I trust that you know what you're doing," Kristen says. "Léoan adores you, and it totally shows."

"I adore him, too." But I really miss him right now.

Nancy opens her office door and yells, "Sweeps!"

"Okay, wicked stepmother," Kristen murmurs under her breath.

ONCE HOME, WHAT NANCY SAID KEEPS PLAYING through my head. Do I really know Léoan the way I think I do? I have the next two days off, so I either explore this or let it go. What if I find out something that I don't want to know? After Ace, I should be vetting guys better, but I don't get an untrustworthy vibe from him at all.

Curiosity gets the best of me, so I pop open my laptop and Google his name. Nothing comes up, at first. It's like Léoan doesn't exist. There is not one trace of him on any social media platform. That's not a surprise because getting to know him these past couple of months, I've learned that he's more old-school. He doesn't do social media and rarely uses his cellphone. At least not when he's around me, which is every waking moment.

He doesn't talk much about himself, either. How can I find anything on him if he has no trail whatsoever? My dad knows some investigators, but do I really want to ask him to check out Léoan? He will probably tell Meg, and I do not want her to know any more of my business. My father can't keep his mouth shut with her. Every little thing that happens to me, he blabs it to her, even when I tell him not to.

I close the laptop. I trust Léoan. More than I've trusted anyone. I don't need to do any of that. He's the best man I have ever met, apart from my dad. Spending time with him has been nothing short of amazing. I don't think he would lie to me and if he did, there would be a good reason. He's at work right now, I reassure myself.

I go to the bathroom and turn on the shower. It's time for me to face my fears by myself. Since Léoan has been gone, I can count on one hand how many showers I have taken. It has become harder for me to be around water, but he usually helps me get through it. I just wish this feeling would go away. I wish I weren't scared like this. I undress, inhale and exhale, then get in the shower. The fear is there, right away, so I wash for a minute and hop out, turning the water off as I exit. I am so exhausted of feeling this way.

Come home soon, Léoan.

17

Léoan

~~~~~~~

"Shannon? Shannon? Can you hear me? Shannon?"

My blurry sight clears and there's a woman looking at me. I look around from left to right and notice I'm in a small room with a bookshelf, tan carpet, a desk, couch, and a couple of chairs. I look down at my hands and realize that they are bound to the arms of the chair. I try to pull them up, but they won't budge.

"I'm Dr. Bryant," a gray-haired woman says. "You've been restrained for your and our safety. You're at the Central Prison, in the mental health facility. You were assigned to me. Tell me, Shannon, do you know who and where you are?"

"Who's Shannon?" I ask. "I'm not Shannon. I'm Homer!"

"You're Homer? Homer who?"

"You're a doctor. I'm sure you've heard of me. What do the history books call me? A writer, a poet, and a philosopher."

"You're telling me that you are Homer, the poet, and philosopher? Back at the jailhouse, you said you were Sir Braveheart."

My memory is a bit fuzzy, and I chuckle because I don't exactly remember doing that, but I do know why I did it. It wasn't because I thought I was Sir Braveheart. I prefer the loony bin over jail cells. It's so much nicer.
~~~~~~~

"Shannon, do you know why you are here?"

"Please stop calling me Shannon. I don't know who that lady is."

"Shannon is your name. We found you in the system, and you had warrants for your arrest, and you've had mental health issues in the past ..."

I drift back off into la-la land as she talks. She gets further away from me, and everything becomes a blur.

"Shannon!" Dr. Bryant yells, plucking me out of the abyss I was diving into.

"Look, my name is Homer, and I am here to find and protect the love of my life!"

"Okay, Homer," Dr. Brant says sarcastically. "Tell me about yourself."

"What do you want to know?"

"I want to know whatever you want to tell me and how you truly think you're someone who died nearly three millennia ago."

"Give or take. And I truly never died, Dr. Bryant. Poseidon made sure of that."

"The god of water? That Poseidon?"

I nod. "I've heard he's going by Neptune, his Roman name. Sounds more ... edgy. I am what I am because of a little thing called ambrosia, given to me by him."

Dr. Bryant removes her eyeglasses and massages her temples. She's clearly aggravated. "You have an interesting arrest record. Domestic violence, grand theft auto, stealing steaks out of Walmart, and now, assault and battery. Oh, how the mighty hath fallen."

She's funny. "I usually don't assault. I murder."

Dr. Bryant is stunned. "Excuse me?"

'I murder."

"How many people have you murdered?" she asks.

"So many, I can't recall, Doc, but each and every one was for a great cause."

"And what cause is that?" Dr. Bryant asks.

"Love."

"You kill people for love? That doesn't sound very loving to me."

"I have no choice."

"I find that very hard to believe," she says.

"Yet, it is true. I haven't always been like this, but given the situation I was in, I had to do something." I lean forward as far as I can. "You know, it's really amazing what a curse mixed with a powerful fruit can do."

"Tell me about it," she says, snapping a pin then resting a clipboard on her lap.

It's a well-known fact that Neptune loathes Odysseus. He's made no attempt to hide it. I suppose I was his guinea pig. I became privy to their sick games of who's dick was bigger, but I had no choice but to appease Neptune. I was cursed by Althea."

"Slow down. You said Odysseus, King of Ithaca?"

"Also known as Ulysses." I smile. "You know your history."

Dr. Bryant rolls her eyes.

"Althea was the Siren I was in lust with. Since lust doesn't last and usually comes to a messy end, and messy it was, I fell madly in love with Sera. Althea didn't take that very well, so she killed Sera and turned me into an ugly fish. A ghost shark to be exact."

"A Siren turned you into a fish."

"Yes. Sirens are half-human, half-bird but many of them take after their father in the way that they can shapeshift. Althea's form of choice was of a mermaid. She was like a mermaid on methamphetamines. Extremely sexual and exorbitantly territorial. I had to study my condition before concluding that I have chimerism. It's common among Ghost Sharks."

"This is all a very elaborate story but ..."

"I was in Althea's grasp for an exceedingly long time before I was able to get away from her. That's when I asked Neptune for help in exchange for the whereabouts of all of the writings and notes I took on voyages with Odysseus. He wanted to know everything Odysseus had been up to— where he'd gone, who he'd met, who he fucked, what he ate and when he shit. Neptune was really obsessed if you ask me. But that obsession granted me freedom from that slippery, slimy shell that Althea had me encased in."

"Let me guess. You're referring to *The Odyssey*?"

She's keeping up. I'm proud of her.

"Neptune warned me. He did not know how the ambrosia would affect me since I was cursed. He was right to warn me, but I didn't listen. I ingested the ambrosia, and although it was delectable, it made me become something ... otherworldly."

"Which is?" Dr. Bryant asks.

"The ambrosia gave me immortality, but it also did something else. It made me into a monster, with an insatiable appetite for blood. Couple that with chimerism, and you get me. At times I don't consider immortality a gift—more like another curse over top of the curse I already suffer from. But, once I found out that Sera was also in a way, immortal, I had something to live forever for. She wasn't dead and gone. She was just being reincarnated. I believe that was a curse given to her by Althea. Althea just couldn't kill her. No, that would have been too easy. She wanted Sera to suffer as much as I did—as much as I *do*."

"You think you're a vampire with ... chim—?"

"Chimerism, correct, yes, but mostly in terms of DNA. I wouldn't classify myself as a vampire either, especially now, because I no longer crave blood, I just need it every few months to survive. Now, my chimerism is what makes me turn into the people I kill. I don't have a choice with that. If I feed, I must kill and in turn, I become them.

"This is outrageous," she sighs, exasperated.

Sorry Doc, but that is the best way to explain my ... condition. 'Vampire' is such a generic term. I don't really identify as a vampire because the only similarity between me and them is the consumption of blood. I no longer crave blood, I can go out in sunlight, and I'm not susceptible to any other things they are susceptible to."

"Then what are you?" she asks.

"I'm a mutt. I wish there was a name for it."

She adjusts her glasses and writes down more notes. "This is all remarkably interesting, Shannon, and I hate to burst your bubble, but you are not a vampire, you are not a Chimera, you are a human being who's in need of mental help. And we are here to help you."

"It's too bad that you don't believe me, Doc, because when I turn back into my true self, I might have to kill you to get out of this place."

Dr. Bryant looks at me over top of her glasses. "You're threatening to kill me?"

"Again, I don't kill people for no reason. Getting out of here is a great reason to kill you."

She presses a button on her walkie-talkie, "Come get Shannon Higgins, please. He just threatened to kill me, over."

Within seconds, an orderly and a couple of guards rush through the door at me. The orderly pierces me with a needle full of God knows what, and the guards roughly wheel me out of Dr. Bryant's office.

The heavyset guard gets extra physical and punches me in the face, giving me a fat lip. "Don't you ever threaten anyone in here ever again, or next time, you'll have more than a bloody lip!"

I guess I won't be killing Dr. Bryant after all.

I WAKE UP LATER IN THE RECREATION ROOM NEXT to a guy staring at me and holding a weathered teddy bear in his lap. How I got here, I don't know. They've been pumping me full of drugs since I arrived.

"You're awake," the bear's owner says.

I look at him and put his age to be in the early twenties. And here he is snuggled up with a stuffed animal. Great. "Unfortunately."

He wipes his nose and giggles. "I'm Tommy, but you can call me Tommy." He offers up a snotty hand.

I wave at him, "Hey."

"You don't look crazy to me," Tommy says and laughs.

"Don't tell them that," I say.

He grabs his teddy bear and talks to it. "Does he look crazy to you?" Then he puts the bear's mouth up to his ear, shaking his stringy brown hair as if the bear is giving him an answer.

"He doesn't think you're crazy either. Just different. And you're hurt. That's why you try to cover up the pain." He looks at my arms, which have track marks all up and down them.

I pull down the sleeve of my itchy thermal I'm wearing underneath the green jumpsuit. "Okay, so you're perceptive." Way more than I was when I chose this body.

"Can you watch Arnold while I go to the bathroom? I trust you. I know the others will try to steal him because he has magical powers."

"Magical powers?"

"Yes. If you hold Arnold, he can make you invisible, but only if you ask."

"Then I guess you're here because you want to be. I mean, surely if Arnold could turn you invisible, you could walk right out of this place."

Tommy shakes his head. "No, I don't want to leave. I like it here. There are scary people outside. I don't want to go outside anymore."

Well, he's not lying. There are scary people outside. "Sure." I agree to babysit Arnold.

"Be good, Arnold," he says excitedly before shoving the bear in my lap and skipping away, his baggy tan pants hanging loosely on his legs.

"K," I say. I really gotta get out of here. I'm babysitting a teddy bear for a grown man.

Tommy skips past the guard that sucker-punched me.

The guard walks to me and stops, a smirk crossing his sweaty face as he grabs his belt, pulling up his ill-fitting pants on top of his protruding belly. He laughs when he sees me sitting there with Arnold in my lap.

I bite my tongue, hard, because if I bite him, I will be thrown in the white room, and I don't want that.

"You look like a proud momma," the guard says, and he laughs some more.

I point at his stomach. "So do you. When is the baby due?"

"You're a comedian, huh?" he says, clearly pissed at my harmless joke. His buddy calls for him, and he shuffles away, breathing heavier with every step.

Tommy returns and plops down in the seat next to me.

I hand him Arnold.

"Were you a good boy?" he asks Arnold.

"Tommy, why are you in here?" I really want to know why this dude is in here. He doesn't look like he can hurt a fly.

"I gave my parents mercy," he says.

"Mercy?"

"Yes. I released them from their cruel lives."

"You killed your parents?"

"No, I didn't kill them. They were having a tough time being good people, so I gave them mercy." He smiles at me.

"They were bad people?"

"Yes, especially my dad. He was scary. He would get angry and hit me all the time. One time I had to stay home from school for a month until the bruises went away. My mom told me that he was having a hard time being a good person."

"Then why didn't you just kill your dad? Why did you kill your mom, too?"

"Because she would be lonely without dad. She told me herself that if I told anyone what my dad did, people would take him away and she would be lonely without him. So, I made sure they stayed together."

"Who gave you the teddy bear?"

'My grandma. She found him in the old house and brought him to me. I named him after my grandpa. He was a nice person. Not mean like my dad. He used to take me fishing a lot before he died."

"How long have you been here?" I ask.

"Six years."

"Sorry to hear that."

"Sometimes I worry about my grandma being around scary people out there. Those people need mercy. Guard Moreno needs mercy. He reminds me of my dad." Tommy points to the rotund man who has been a thorn in my side.

"I can't disagree with that."

"He hits me sometimes, and he tries to steal Arnold from me. He's not nice person."

"He really isn't, but people are going to be what they are," I say. "Some people are good, some are bad. You can't just kill those you deem bad people." I am the biggest hypocrite this side of the Carolina River.

"That's why me and Arnold stay here. Away from the bad people."

I look over at Mr. Moreno, who's staring at me again. I narrow my eyes and he returns the sentiment and straightens his back.

He is so lucky I'm humaning.

BREAKFAST IN THIS PLACE TASTES LIKE T.V. DINNERS from the seventies. I've been here for eight days, and I'm still not used to this slop. I gag as I choke down the powdered eggs and tough turkey bacon haphazardly thrown onto a beige plastic plate. Normally, when I am humaning, I get food that I know to be delicious, since I don't need food in my normal form. But if I'm in a situation where I have to eat what is given to me, that's definitely a downside. I grab a piece of burnt toast and lose a fingernail that falls on the platter. Then I bite into the bread, and I'm crunching on more than burnt toast.

Shit. It's happening! Why does this always occur when I'm in the middle of doing something? And on top of that, it's early. Lately, it never happens when I'm asleep or alone. That would be way too convenient. I look around and quickly get up and race to my room, but I'm not alone, Mr. tough guy bully guard follows behind me.

"Breakfast isn't over yet," Moreno says. "Where do you think you're going?"

I ignore him, veer left, and run into the bathroom. I go into a stall and hop on the toilet, standing on the lid, squatting while I shed this form.

Moreno bursts inside. "Return to the eating area now!"

I didn't want to do this, but now I do. I'll be doing everyone here a favor.

He looks under the stall and all he sees is a heap of ashes. "What the fuck?"

I kick the door off the hinges sending him careening into the bathroom wall. He's baffled and trying to grasp what's happening to him and who the fuck I am when I walk up to him.

"You really followed me in here? I could have had the shits or had to puke or anything. I think you have a crush on me, to be honest."

Moreno reaches for his Taser, but I kick it out of his hand. "You could have left well enough alone, but you've been on my ass since I got here. Now you have played into this little scheme of mine perfectly, and I didn't even know you would be in the cast of characters."

"Who are you?" he asks.

"I'm you." I lunge at him.

He sprays me with pepper spray, and I pull away from him, coughing and crying. "My eyes!" I shout. "No! You got me!"

Moreno leaps up just as I lunge forward again, this time stopping two inches from his face and smiling because he made his own bed. He asked for this and now he's getting exactly what he asked for. He will never beat anyone again.

"Help!" he yells.

I put my hand over his mouth and devour him, depleting his wretched soul of life. When I'm done, I jam the entrance shut, drag him into a stall, then take off his clothes and put them on myself being sure I get the whole ensemble because it's almost showtime.

I walk through the prison, passing Tommy who stares at me as if he knows, and right out the front gates in two minutes tops. Looking behind me, I pause and sniff the fresh air of freedom. I'm never going back there again.

Now to go see my baby ...

By the time I get to the main road, I'm out of breath. I stop and sit on a bench at the bus stop. This is going to be hard! I'm going to have to be this piece of shit for a while but killing him was worth it and I'd do it again in a heartbeat. I go through his wallet and find bus fare just as the bus pulls up and I'm on my way home.

Home is where the heart is.

18

Léoan

There my baby is. I watch as Samia passes by. I am at the public computers, pretending to be browsing. Could I have waited to see her? Yes, of course, but did I want to wait? Hell no! I miss her. I miss her curves, her voice, her hair...*everything*. It makes my soul all right even though my soul is currently stuck in a five hundred pound forty-something-year-old balding man. I got a rental car since mine is in police custody. I'll have to go get that later. I wonder what they will say to me. "Yeah, we thought you were dead, and the guy who allegedly killed you disappeared out of the prison psycho unit!"

As I'm thinking of this, my eyes follow Samia's every move section by section, watching her help customer after customer and watching her interact with them. That smile— it's a genuine one. I love when she smiles like that, and I bask in the glory that I'm the one who makes that smile happen.

Kristen picks up the loudspeaker and announces that the library will be closing in five minutes. I exit and head to my car. Someone calls me from a dark corner of the building.

"Homer?" The person laughs. "Is that you? You look absolutely disgusting."

A form emerges from the shadow. Nancy? I look at her shocked. She laughs, then sucks on a cigarette.

"You just called me Homer," I say.

"That I did," Nancy responds.

"May I ask why you called me that?"

"Because that's who you are."

"I don't' know what you think you know, but you're wrong. I don't know who Homer is."

"You do know who he is because you are him," Nancy says.

"Is that so? Enlighten me."

"I know you, Homer. You may not know me, but I know you." She walks closer, throws her cigarette on the ground, and stamps it out. "I'll let you marinate on that."

She tries to pass by me, but I grab her arm. Not so fast. "You're not going to say something like this and just walk away. Who are you? Why are you calling me that?" My patience is wearing thin from this sick game she's playing.

She looks down at my hand and at me. "What are you going to do to me if I don't tell you? Hmm? Surely, you're not going to hurt me here. Not in front of your little girlfriend. She might find out about the monster you really are. I'll throw you a bone, though. I have a sister who's angry with you, and it's only a matter of time before you feel her wrath again." She pulls her arm from me. "You should leave Samia alone."

"And if I don't?"

"History will most definitely repeat itself." She sees the expression on my face turn from anger to fear, and she laughs. "We can't all have what we want and trust me when I say that you will never have what *you* want."

She knows who I am and how she knows, I have no idea. Before coming to this library, I'd never seen her before in my entire life. She needs to talk. Now! I stop her again and grab her around her scrawny neck just when Samia and Kristen come around the corner and see me standing there.

"What the fuck are you doing!" Kristen yells. "Let her go!"

Samia starts rummaging through her purse, and I know she's getting some kind of weapon out of it. That's when I bolt to my car and burn rubber out of there. This has Althea written all over it. Nancy even admitted she was her sister.

Fuck! Now what? Do I tell Samia? I have no choice. She has to know the truth. I think Samia is in danger. I knew there was something "off" about Nancy, and I have the feeling she's not above doing the absolute worst to Samia. Althea really took to heart the saying "Keep your enemies closer." After all these years, she's still a bitter Betty, or better yet, a miserable old bird.

I park outside of Samia's apartment. When she pulls in and goes inside, I rush upstairs and knock on the door while looking down at myself and not being able to see my feet because my belly is in the way. She's never going to believe me! No, she has to believe me. Her life depends on it!

19

Samia

There's a knock at the door seconds after I get home. I look through the peephole and see it's the same man that attacked Nancy! My heart immediately starts racing. He must have followed me!

"I'm calling the police! Go away!" I wish Léoan was here to protect me!

"Samia, we need to talk," he says, his voice muffled through the door.

"How do you know my name?" I run to my purse and grab my pepper spray, Taser, and cell and get ready to dial 911.

"Samia, please. I just need ... to ... do it ... scared. Please, give me..."

Oh my God! He's begging to rape me and wants me to be scared while he's doing it! "They're on their way!" I shakily unlock my phone and press the nine.

"It's me! Léoan!"

I hesitate over the number 1. "How do you know Léoan?"

"I am Léoan!" he yells.

"What?" My phone rings. Léoan is calling me. I answer and say, "Léoan! I'm in trouble!"

"No, you're not."

The voice comes from the other side of my door! "How do you have my boyfriend's phone? What did you do to him?"

"Samia, please listen to me," he begs. "I am your boyfriend. I am Léoan, I swear to you, I am. It's a long story, and I know it's going to sound unbelievable, but I need you to listen to me, and you have to believe me because I th nk your life is in danger."

"You're crazy! You expect me to believe that you are my boyfriend? Unless you got a voice change and you put on a fat suit, there is no explanation for this at all. Even then it would be a very questionable one. Tell it to the police." I get ready to hang up on him and dial 9-1-1.

"Please, Samia! Your parents live in Bald Head Island, and you have a dog named Bo, and ... we met at your job. Your best friend is Kristen, and you love metal music but don't really tell anyone, not even Ace. I know that umm ..I know that you didn't love Ace, but you used him to scare the bad things away. You feel the most comfortable around books, and at times, you are deathly afraid of water. Except for those times when I shower with you and we sit in the bathtub and I help you detangle your beautiful, kinky, and stubborn hair. And ... when you sleep, sometimes you have bad dreams, and I wish to God I could fix that for you. I want to fix everything. What I did in the past, this is all my fault and I'm so, so sorry." His voice cracks. "But I love you more than anything, Samia. You are my life."

"How do you know those things?"

"Just don't hang up, Samia, okay? I will tell you everything...just give me a chance. Please."

Some things he could have easily found out from Léoan, but the other stuff? I wonder why Léoan would tell anyone those things. They are insignificant. I can hear the desperation in his voice, but I can't be too careful.

"I'm listening," I say.

"I ... I have loved you a long time, Samia. You used to be called Sera. That used to be your name when we first met eons ago. Ancient Greece. The moment I laid eyes on you in that ship, my entire world changed. You cast light through the dark, mundane life I was living. You gave me a real reason to believe that I had a future. You were pregnant when you were killed."

"What are you talking about? Ancient Greece? I was pregnant when I was killed?"

"Yes, Samia, it's all true, and Nancy ties into all this, but I have yet to figure out how."

"Nancy?"

"That's why you saw what you saw. She is a danger to you, Samia. I think she is aligned with Althea."

"Wait, who's Althea?"

"Althea is who killed you and my baby. You were drowned. That's why you're so afraid of water."

I hang up the phone and swing the door open.

He looks relieved.

"Come in," I order.

He walks through the door then sighs and starts to turn around. "Thank you so much—"

I spray him and tase the shit out of him.

He collapses, making a loud bang as he hits the floor.

AFTER SUCCESSFULLY ZIP-TYING HIS HANDS together, I get a bottled water and dump it on his head. He wakes up, startled, coughing and trying to adjust his eyes.

"You could have killed me, Samia."

"And?" I say.

He gasps, "This isn't the kind of body that can handle being tased like that." He blinks rapidly. "You pepper sprayed me too? Great? Used your entire arsenal on me, I see. At least you didn't shoot—"

I pull the gun from behind my back and wave him over to a chair. "Get up and sit there. I couldn't move your big ass while you were passed out. 'C'mon. Chop chop."

He crawls on his knees to the chair, where he slightly lifts himself up and sits.

Then I duct tape him to the chair. Tightly.

"Really, Samia? This isn't necessary."

"It is very necessary. You're a strange man claiming to be my boyfriend, yet you are somehow in another man's body. And you said I was murdered eons ago, and I can't fathom why I believed you enough for you to get this far. But 'm listening."

"Let me start from the beginning."

"By all means," I say, as I sit on the coffee table facing him. "Let's start with how you have Léoan's phone and how you know all those things that only he and I know. Did you talk to him and steal his phone, or did you do something to him?"

"Mia, I am Léoan! I don't know how many times I have to say it!'

"Excuse me?" Umm, hello?" I wave the gun around again. "I'm the one holding the gun. I'm the one with the power. Capisce?"

"I capisce," he agrees, his eyes red and bulging from the spray.

I go to the kitchen and pour a glass of wine. If I'm going to hear him out, I'm going to need something. I return to the coffee table, cross my legs and stare at him. "Now, go on.'

"You already look like you don't believe me," he says.

"That assumption would be correct, but please, continue." I take a gulp of Moscato.

"Continuing from what I said before, we met in the year twelve B.C."

"Twelve B.C.? As in Before Christ? That BC?"

"Yes, that B.C. I am Homer."

"The philosopher?"

He nods.

"But Homer was like sixty something when he died Why are you so young?"

"Because I wasn't that old. If you haven't noticed, everything about me is a mystery. My birth and death are estimations. Only I know the truth. People have made up their own tales about me."

I sit there as he explains how he can turn into other people. I'm refilling my glass as I'm listening, and this all sounds ridiculous but nevertheless, I hear him out. This is better than any fiction book I've ever read.

"Althea was a Siren that I was smashing. It wasn't love, it was lust, but she felt she owned me. I was on a voyage with Odysseus when I met you, stowed away, running away from your family. I helped you hide throughout the journey, and we fell in love. From that point on we were inseparable. I got us a house in Nikaia. We were so happy. You got pregnant. We were going to extend our family. Everything was perfect, until—"

"Althea," I interrupt.

"Yes." He puts his head down. "She had a beautiful voice, and with that voice, she called you down to the shore. That's when she drowned you and our baby. Then she cursed me to live a life of looking at her fishy tail for eternity."

"If she killed me, then why am I here? Where is the baby?"

"My guess is that she cursed you, too, because you are being reincarnated over and over again." He looks intently in my eyes. "Samia, this isn't the first time I've found you. I found you at least a dozen other times."

"Was I me? What did I look like?"

"Last time I found you, you were a man."

"What?"

"Yes. But that's how reincarnation works. The shell changes but the soul stays the same. I can sense it. That's how I keep finding you."

"Did you...did you have sex with me?"

He nods.

"So, I was a gay man in my past life?"

"Well, umm, you actually weren't, but you were with me."

"I was only gay with you? Do you hear yourself right now?"

"It sounds crazy, but yeah. I mean, you had a wife and kids and it just ... happened."

"Wait!" I almost choke on my wine. "I was married and you were my side dude?"

"Pretty much." He shrugs.

"Homewrecker."

"I'll wreck a thousand homes just to be with you. Sorry. Not really, though. You *are* my home."

I stare at him. This is definitely something Léoan would say.

"Hey, look at it this way," he continues. "You know it's true love when you're bending over a dead ringer for Mario from Mario Brothers. Your soul shined through despite all of that. It was just a shell. We were together for two weeks before you died. Hit by a bus. Yeah, it was messy."

"What about the other times?" I ask.

"It varied in every case. The only thing that stays the same is your soul, and I always find you when you're twenty-six years old. That's the age you were when Althea killed you, and that's also the age when you die. It usually happens right in front of me. Rarely when I'm humaning."

"Humaning?"

"Yes, that's what I call it. This world is a very big place, Samia. I have traveled to the ends of the earth to find you, only to lose you repeatedly."

"So, if I die ... again ... I will come back as another person, and you will find me again."

"That's usually how it works, but one thing that's different, out of all the times I've been with you, you never had déjà vu, déjà rêvé, or night terrors. I think it's you trying to remember and your brain is fighting against it."

"So, what happens if I do remember? When the memories come flooding in and I wake up like I'm awaking from the Matrix. What happens then?"

"I don't know," he replies. "It's never happened before."

"Answer me this," I say, kneeling in front of him. "If I die as soon as you find me, then why do you keep trying to find me?"

"Because I'm selfish! I want you, Samia! Always!"

"Well, obviously, your wanting is dangerous to me! You're putting your wants and needs before my very existence!"

He throws his head back and closes his eyes.

"I guess the truth hurts," I say.

"Look, Samia. This all has to change. We can't keep going through this."

"Ya think? How did you get in this body? Do you have to kill the people? Did you kill this guy?"

"Yes, I did," he replies. "But only because I was locked up in a prison mental ward I was never going to get out of. I had to do it."

"How did you kill him?"

"I ... drank his blood."

"Okay, so you're a vampire? She cursed you with vampirism?"

"No, she turned me into a fish, but the ambrosia I ingested gave me back my body but added a vampiric ability along with immortality. Neptune bartered with it for my writings. I think we should find Neptune when I'm myself again. He may know how to break the curses. I've been tracking him. He moves around a lot. Even more than me."

"The King of the Sea?"

He nods.

"Well, why not, eh? You can drink blood, shift forms, and you're immortal. Why not know an immortal god, too?" I go to the kitchen and refill my glass. "How many people have you killed?"

"More than I can count," he replies.

I walk out and stand in front of him. "Did you kill, Ace?"

He looks down at the floor.

"Did you. Kill. Ace?"

He stays silent.

"Answer me!"

"Yes, I did, but—"

I tase him, knocking him out cold again, then go into my room and cry myself to sleep.

"GOOD MORNING," HE SAYS AS I PASS BY HIM HEADED to the kitchen. "Sleep well?"

"What do you think?" I scoff.

"I slept well after you hit me with fifty thousand volts of pure electrical energy."

I stop and give him a wry smile. "There's more where that came from."

"Oh, baby. Don't threaten me with a good time."

I roll my eyes as I get a skillet and set it on the stove. "Are you hungry? Never mind, of course you are."

"Are you fat shaming me? I'm actually on a diet, thank you very much."

"I'm not fat, and I'm hungry. Am I fat-shaming myself? Besides, if you're going to be leaving that body, why do you bother taking care of it?"

"For one, I have to live in it, and for two—"

"It's your way of saying sorry to the person you've killed," I interrupt.

"I wouldn't say all that ..."

"Think about it. What's really the point?"

"It's become a ritual." He clears his throat uncomfortably.

"Ritual, smitual. Just say you feel bad for murdering them." I crack eggs in a bowl, mix them, and throw them into my favorite non-stick skillet.

"I try, for the most part, to be a decent human being when I'm humaning. There are so few decent humans out here."

"I can't argue with you about that."

I make two pieces of toast and slice some tomato and put them on the plate with the scrambled eggs. When I walk to him, I can't help but feel bad for him. He's there all duct-taped and looking so pitiful. "Here." I shove a forkful of eggs at him as he turns his head from side to side avoiding it. "Ahhhhh," I say. "Don't make me do choo-choo trains."

"Samia, I'm not hungry. I feel like shit, to be honest."

"Open wide. Ahhhh ..."

"Samia, stop."

"Here comes the choo train. Chugga, chugga, chugga, choo, choo." The fork lands on his pressed lips.

"Samia, please!"

I back away from him as he starts shaking. "What's going on?"

"I think I'm turning back. It's too early!"

"Oh, my God! What should I do!"

"Release me! I don't want you to see me like this!"

I run and grab scissors out of the kitchen then try to cut his restraints. "Stop moving!"

"I can't!" he yells.

I watch as he twists and turns and contorts into shapes I've never seen. His body looks like a blowup doll someone popped and is now shriveling. Léoan emerges like a snake shedding its skin. When the residue from the old body hits the ground, it instantly turns to ash. Soon, I stare at Léoan sitting in the chair naked. He snaps the twist ties and tears the duct tape with one motion.

I drop the plate and back away, my eyes as large as saucers as his gorgeous body walks to me dusting off remnants of shedding like a miner dusting off a priceless gem. He embraces me and kisses me on the forehead.

"I can't believe I'm hugging you after what I just witnessed," I whisper.

"I call it metamorphosis ... like body exfoliation."

"Exfoliation." I don't argue, how could I? I just saw my boyfriend change skin. I'm speechless.

"I'm going to take a shower."

He walks away leaving me standing in the room still stunned. He told me about it, but I didn't think I would actually see it. I suppose it wasn't as bad as I imagined, but it was still kind of bad. How many women can say their man can do that? I guess I'm special? Or I've always found myself in the weirdest of situations my entire life. I'm seeing more and more what he said about me ... about my reincarnation .. is unbelievable but true.

Aren't I the special one?

20

Léoan

~~~~~~~~~

I didn't want Samia to see that. Not to mention I shed that body way too quickly. I wasn't that man for a week. It may be the multiple tasings I endured, but I can't be sure. I let the water run down the top of my head and down my body, washing away the last remnants of a very dirty prison guard.

I don't blame her for freaking out. I would do the same thing if the tables were turned and some strange woman came to me saying she was Samia.

Just as I'm formulating how to bring her back to reality and absorbing what she just saw, the shower curtain opens and she is standing there, staring at me. I stare back at her. I am usually never at a loss for words, but right now, I don't know what to say. She slips out of her maroon spaghetti-strapped tank and snowman patterned pajama bottoms and gets in with me, embracing me from behind, her soft breasts pressing against my back. Then she rests her head on my back as I cup my hands over hers and squeeze them.

"About Ace—"

"I know why you did it," she whispers. "You did it for me."

"Everything I have done and will do is for you. It's all for you. I love you, Ser, no, I love you, Samia."

"Please don't kill anyone again," she says.
~~~~~~~~~

"This has gone on for too long. I should have fixed it sooner. I've been complacent because I just wanted to be with you, but it's clear Althea will never let us live in peace. This is all my fault."

"How can it be all your fault if you met Althea before we met?"

"I know but—" I put my head down.

"This is her fault and hers alone. You're here now, Léoan. I've missed you so much."

I turn, cradle her chin, and bring her lips to mine, kissing them softly, savoring the salty sweetness. "I've missed these lips."

She kisses me back, our tongues playing back and forth like a bow stroking violin strings in a perfectly conducted orchestra. She places her hand on my cheek and looks at me, caressing my bottom lip with her thumb.

Goosebumps ripple up and down my spine as I close my eyes then suck on her thumb. I pick her up, and she wraps her shiny mocha legs around my waist. I grip her ass with one hand while I guide myself into her with the other, then I stop there and feel the warmth encase me, gripping my firm cock as if holding on for dear life.

She whispers in my ear "I love you, too," placing her arms around my neck as I pump, our lips glued together, each one of us swallowing one another's gratuitous, muffled moans as they are released. Her breasts slide up and down my chest as I move, each stroke tuning us, bringing us in sync with one another. I moan with her, louder and louder until her walls squeeze me something fierce and she starts convulsing, letting out a pleasurable scream. That's when I unload everything that's been building up in me for days, missing being inside of her, missing her touch, her smell, her voice. I come harder and louder than I ever have before, steadying myself with one arm on the shower wall. We stay in this position and come back down to earth together.

After round three, we lie in bed next to each other, just the hallway light illuminating parts of us. I could live like this. I could live in this bed with her for the rest of time.

"What do we do now?" she asks, using her forefinger to make little imaginary circles on my chest.

"We talk to Neptune. He knows pretty much everything. And who better to tell me the secret then the actual King of the Sea?"

"When are you going?" she asks.

"We are going soon. I've been tracking his whereabouts, and he should be somewhere here in the United States."

"I can't go. I have to work."

"Samia, you can't go back there. I don't trust Nancy. She is not who she pretends to be."

"Léoan, I do have a life. I can't just stop everything. Besides, I love my job."

"Babe, I've got more money than you can imagine. You can get another job later. I must try to make things right."

"Léoan, I—" She holds her mouth and races to the bathroom.

I hear her retching in the toilet. After getting to the bathroom, I see her sitting against the bathtub basin with her head on her knees, and her arms wrapped around her legs.

"Are you okay?" I ask.

"Yeah, my stomach is just queasy. It will go away."

I kneel down as she looks at me. "I know this has been a lot to take in and I'm sorry, but you need to understand you can't go back to work yet. Please be patient and let me fix this—let me fix *us*."

She nods.

I pick her up and carry her back to bed where she falls asleep almost instantly. I slip away and go to the living room to use her laptop to try to track exactly where Neptune is right now. It's sitting on the coffee table with her notebook on top of it. I'll just take a quick peek inside.

It's like (The Real Thing)

When he smiles, I feel like better things are possible
Like him loving me is not just a dream, but plausible
It's like he's optimistic enough for the both of us
And when I hear his heart beating like a symphonic melody, I feel unstoppable!
Like it's not just a great love, it's phenomenal
Like dead leaves falling from trees is incredible
Knowing they're making room for new life, a joy that's indescribable
Resting in his arms is like having on headphones in a secure bubble
He proved me wrong when I thought I was unlovable
He pulls me out from the rubble, endangering his whole being
Seizes my fears, and loves me until I am comfortable
He changed me from a colorless zombie to a vibrant sentient being
It's like he's rubbing off on me, the good sans the bad and the ugly
It's like a real thing I didn't need, want or envy.
But it's what was missing.
It's like a dream ...

My baby finally wrote about me.
And I can't stop smiling.

21

Samia

Léoan and I make the eight-hour drive to New York City in seven and a half. I'm spent once we get to the St. Regis Hotel. Walking into our room, I gasp at the grand chandeliers dangling from the ceiling that has to be at least ten feet high.

"This is amazing!" I squeal as I get lost looking at all the rooms. The kitchen and dining areas are massive, nothing like my apartment's kitchen. "I've never stayed anywhere so fancy. I almost don't want to touch anything."

"Well, you can touch me." Léoan winks at me.

"I plan to," I quip and stick out my tongue.

"We should really try out the bed," he suggests.

"Agreed." I peek into the bathroom that's as big as an average master bedroom. It's all adorned in marble made into artistic shapes. "Exquisite."

"TAO nightclub is only twenty-three minutes from here," Léoan says from the bedroom.

"What if he's not here?"

"Trust me, he is. He's just gotten to this area. It's Turn Up Tuesday there, and he's never one to miss a party."

"But I thought you said he moves a lot."

"Moving a lot for immortals is moving every decade or so. He will probably stay about ten years. Give or take."

I unpack my stuff—including all my weapons and lay them on the bed. He wraps me in his arms. "Babe?"

"Yes?" I look up at him.

"You don't need those with me around." He kisses me on the forehead.

"I know, but I feel better having them with me. Just a habit, I guess."

"You're such a badass,"

"I'm a badass chick with a sexy Greek immortal sweetheart, that's for sure."

WHEN WE ARRIVE AT TAO NIGHTCLUB, LÉOAN SPOTS Neptune quickly. That man would be damn near impossible to miss. I'm blinded by the long platinum beard that clings to his clear, albino-like complexion. His ocean-blue eyes pop when he sees us approaching him.

"Long time, no see." Neptune stands and pats Léoan on the back.

"I wish it was under better circumstances," Léoan says.

Neptune looks over at me. I almost get lost in his eyes. I can see the blue current and the white foam move torrentially then come to a stop when he takes my hand and kisses it. Léoan better watch this one.

Neptune sits and smacks two women on the ass that are wearing Geisha makeup and revealing outfits. They look at Léoan and giggle, playfully waving fans back and forth, hiding their faces. I do not like them at all. They lay their heads on Neptune's firm, brawny shoulders, one on each ripped arm.

"I need to find a way to break the curse Althea put on us," Léoan says.

"How am I supposed to know how to do that?" Neptune asks while leaning forward and resting his arms on his knees, staring at Léoan.

"I figured you might know where she is," Léoan says. "Maybe I can reason with her?"

"Reason with Althea?" Neptune laughs. "Homer, how could you mess around with a Siren in the first place? You traveled with Odysseus. I know he warned you about them."

"He did, but—"

"But you didn't listen to Odysseus telling y'all to steer clear of the Sirens. Instead, you were lured in by her enchanting song. Sounds to me like you deserved what happened to you."

"He did, and I didn't listen. I just thought Althea was ... misunderstood."

"Misunderstood? That was a huge misunderstanding because now here you are again eons later still cursed and asking me for help. How's that for a misunderstanding? She really did a number on you." Neptune lets out a long whistle.

"I'm here eons later because you gave me the ambrosia," Léoan says.

"That you asked for. I mean, you could have stayed a shark." Neptune shrugs, and the two women rise off their seats. "You probably would have at least died in a timely manner."

Léoan massages his temples. "But then I wouldn't be able to be with Samia."

"We just want to know if you know how to break the curse, that's all," I interject.

"I assume you have to kill her," Neptune says. "How else would you break a curse? You kill the curser."

"How can I do that when I don't know where she is?" Léoan asks. "Or how to kill her."

"And that's why you've come to me, of course." Neptune sits back and crosses his arms. "Do you know Triton thinks of her as a daughter? Although she's *not* his daughter and her mother lied. But this leaves me in quite the pickle You expect me to sell out my own flesh and blood?"

"You said she's not Triton's blood daughter, though," Léoan says.

"Still, *he* considers her a daughter," Neptune says. "So, I have to take his feelings into consideration, you know?"

"What do you want?" Léoan asks. "Name your price."

Neptune reaches for a wine glass. His rings clang and glisten against it as he looks at me. "What did you say your name was?"

"Samia," I reply. "And I didn't say."

"Ah. Like Maia. Close to the mother of Hermes. In Greek, it translates to mother. Do you have any more children, Samia?"

"Any more? I don't have any." What's with this guy? Is he stereotyping me? Judging by the earlier conversation, he's not a very tolerant person and this coming from the baby daddy of the sea. The nerve!

Neptune looks at me then smiles at Léoan. "I want your firstborn."

Léoan frowns. "What?"

Neptune wrinkles his pointy nose while simultaneously rubbing his beard. "Your firstborn child for the whereabouts of Althea." Neptune casually scoops a handful of peanuts out of a frosted blue buffet jar on the table and pops them into his mouth.

Léoan stands and grabs my hand.

"I'm kidding, I'm kidding." Neptune laughs. "Sit down."

"That's *not* funny, and this is *no* laughing matter," Léoan says as we sit. "Must be nice to be able to laugh about it."

"Althea is as disgraceful as that mother of hers, who at one time tried to trap me in her own little web of deceit. Triton knows this, but he's too pigheaded to listen to reason. He's always been like that. We are not fathers to Sirens. They're birds, for fuck's sake. That's a total disgrace for our family. Although she prances around in mermaid form, she's not fooling me, like she fools everyone else." Neptune stares at Léoan. "No offense.

"Some taken," Léoan says.

"I see her for who she really is," Neptune says. "Hell, a blind man could see that she's trouble. She is the daughter of Aecholes—a river rat. But even he's not claiming her. There is no doubt Althea is his daughter. Sometimes her ilk come to the sea and try to fit in with real mermaids, but we all know they don't belong there."

"That sounds kind of ... speciest," I explain.

"What's that?" Neptune asks.

"It's like racist but against certain species," I say.

"Oh, believe me, I am not 'speciest,'" Neptune says, rolling his eyes. "I have lots of diverse types of friends. Some of my best friends are Sirens."

"What are their names?" Léoan asks with a smirk on his face.

"You don't know them," Neptune mumbles. "They don't get out much."

"Mhm," I moan.

"But, you know, they are into all types of weird shit," Neptune says.

"Who told you that?" Léoan asked. "Your Siren friends?"

Neptune nods then peers at Léoan. "Sirens know magic. That's why she was able to turn you into a shark. Oh, and a very ugly one at that."

"Thanks," Léoan says sarcastically.

"Look, I'll tell you her whereabouts but not for free," Neptune says. "Nothing in life is for free, my friend."

"I've given you the most valuable thing I had for the ambrosia," Léoan says.

"When's the last time you spoke to Odysseus?" Neptune says.

"Too long to remember," Léoan replies.

"Have you written anything else, any ancient texts you may have 'forgotten about' on one of your little voyages?" Neptune asks.

"Look, I gave you the originals, and you turned around and released them to the world. I stopped sailing after I met Sera." Léoan looks at me, smiles, and squeezes my hand.

I love it when he looks at me like that. Total goosebumps, and he's so sincere.

Neptune leans into Léoan. "You're welcome."

"Well, that really didn't do much for me," Léoan says.

"You are a very well-respected historical figure, just like me," Neptune says.

"Okay, but how does that help me in my current situation?" Léoan asks.

"A thank you would be nice." Neptune crosses his arms over his chest like a spoiled kid who has been refused ice cream before supper.

Léoan sighs. "Gee, thanks."

"Look, I don't know where she is at the moment," Neptune says. "Last I heard she was somewhere possibly here in the States. Now you need to ask yourself something. If, as you say, Althea wants to harm Samia, then she would most likely be somewhere closest to her. Keep in mind she's a shifter. She can turn into a human form."

"Tell me how to kill her," Léoan says.

"Look, if she's still alive after all of this time, most likely she can't be killed by mere human means," Neptune says.

Léoan looks at me. "Nancy. It's her. She's Althea."

"Nancy?" I say.

Léoan thanks Neptune, and we are out of there in a flash. When we get back to the hotel room, we figure out what our next move is going to be.

"Nancy lied. She is Althea and she's been here this whole time." Léoan says. "At first I was thinking we were going to have to find her, but she's been sitting right there under our noses."

I gulp. "But ... kill her?"

"Samia, it's either that or she's going to kill you."

"We can't just move away? Like, move to the west coast somewhere. Oh! Or better yet, what about going back to Greece? We will be far away from her."

"I wish it were that simple, but it's not," Léoan says. "It's the only way."

"Yeah, but what happens once she's dead and the curse is lifted off both of us? Will I cease to exist?"

"I'm confident what will happen is that you will be able to live out this life right now and from there, you won't be reincarnated any longer. You will be free from that. No more coming back just to be killed and to come back repeatedly."

"But what happens to you, Léoan? I die and you go on living?"

"No. I'm dying, too."

"What do you mean?" I ask.

"Samia, I love things right now, Althea aside. I love *us* right now. We live our lives out and that's it. When you go, I go, too. I'm almost certain if I don't human, then I will die. If that's not the case, I will just turn into a human and kill myself." He shrugs.

"Léoan!" I give him an incredulous look.

"What?" he replies.

"I can't let you do that!" I nod my head. "Anyway, you're immortal. I thought immortal people couldn't die."

"Being immortal doesn't mean you can't die. It just means if you avoid all the right things, then you can live forever." He lifts my chin. "But you're worth it. I will suffer worse walking this earth without you walking it, too. I will be dead inside anyway."

"But—" Suddenly it feels like my stomach is in my throat. I run to the bathroom, unloading everything I've eaten for the day into the fancy, porcelain commode.

Léoan checks on me. When he walks in, I stare up at him. He instantly knows what that look means.

"You told me you were on the pill," he says.

"I am," I reply. "Never missed one day, but my period is late."

He kneels down in front of me. "I'm sorry. Something like this never crossed my mind. Given what I am, maybe birth control doesn't work against my ... swimming kids."

"I don't know." I shake my head.

"I'll be back," he says, leaving to go to the nearest store.

22

Léoan

I never considered the possibility of Samia becoming pregnant with my child. I'm not opposed to it and never have been. By all means, I welcome it, but I don't know what the baby might be like. Will he or she be normal? I know humans technically aren't normal in any way, shape, or form, but will he or she be ... afflicted ... with my condition?

"What does it say?" I ask anxiously.

Samia comes out of the bathroom and hands me the pregnancy test. Though one line is faint, both lines are pink. "It's positive."

"You're pregnant. Just like when you were Sera." I embrace her harder than I've ever embraced anyone as the realization sets in. At that moment, I also realize that I have to kill Nancy, AKA Althea, as soon as possible. There is no other option left for us. I throw on my jacket and shoes.

"Where are you going?" Samia asks.

"We will never be able to live in peace as long as Althea exists. The sooner I kill her, the sooner we can start planning our future together. But while I'm doing this, I need you to be somewhere safe."

Samia nods. "I'll go stay at my parents. My dad has all kinds of weapons. With his and mine together, we will be fine."

"Okay." I give her my keys. "Take the car. The tank is full, so don't stop anywhere or for anything. Okay? Don't speed so you won't get pulled over by the police. I'll rent a car and meet you at your parent's house after the deed is done."

She embraces me, sliding her arms inside my jacket and wrapping them around my torso. "Please, be careful."

"I promise, I will."

BEFORE I GO BACK TO THE LIBRARY TO END ALTHEA'S existence, I visit TAO one last time, and I am glad that Neptune is still there. This time he's got five women surrounding him. When he sees me approaching him, he snaps his fingers and the women disperse.

"Back so soon?" he asks.

"How do I kill her?" I ask him. "I need to be sure she will never come back."

"You know you're going to be a father, don't you?" Neptune asks.

"I just found out. Now I know what that little stunt of yours was for."

Neptune smiles. "Why do you love her so much still? You've made your entire existence about her. You're immortal. You should be enjoying the perks that come with that."

"I am. Finding Samia is the only perk I need."

He shakes his head. "Let's see here. The way you kill any Siren is easier than you think, and I'm surprised you haven't figured it out yet. Do you remember Odysseus and how he was able to resist them? I don't like the man, but he does have his strong points. When he resisted the Sirens' singing, what did they do? They nose-dived into the ocean, never to be seen again. You know this. You wrote this."

"Yes, but times have changed. That sounds too simple."

"The more things change, the more they stay the same. People change all the time, but they always carry that one thing. That one weakness to something. We all do, whether immortal, mortal, man, woman, or animal. It's all about the ego." He taps a long finger on the side of his head. "Our egos will always be our worst enemy. You spurn a Siren's advance and deny them affection. That grinds their gears."

I get up to leave. "It's been nice seeing you again."

"The feeling is mutual."

He motions for me to come closer to him. "Give me your hand."

I do so, and he puts something in it and closes my hand back up.

"No peeking," Neptune says. "Put this in your pocket and use it when the time is right."

I shove it in my pocket then leave looking back and watching as the women return to throw themselves on him. He might be a player, but that's a very wise man. A man that always gets what he wants and whatever he just gave me is something to help me defeat Althea.

THE NEXT DAY, I GO TO THE LIBRARY JUST BEFORE closing time. I see Nancy through the windows, so I step to the side and wait in a dark corner. Everyone exits, and Nancy's the last one to leave. She locks the door and heads to her car when I grab her and pull her into the corner. As I hold one hand over her mouth, she looks at me startled as I stare at her intently.

She chomps into my hand, pushes me, and tries to run away.

I catch up to her, tackling her to the ground.

"Let go of me!" she yells and bites my fingers.

"I'll let you go all right, but unfortunately, I will have to be you for a while. I'm not happy about that as you are a very unattractive woman but killing you will be the absolute best thing I have ever done, Althea! I don't want you! Once again, I am done with you! There is nothing that would make me want you again!"

She throws her head back and laughs. "I'm not Althea, you fucking fool! I'm her sister! Wrong Siren."

"Liar!"

"She wanted me to keep an eye on your little lover, just in case you showed up again and showed up you did. Just like always. She read you like a book! Althea has your little lovey-dovey. Don't worry. Samia's probably not dead yet. My sister said you like to watch."

"If you're not Althea, then who is she? Tell me where she is!" I yell.

"It must have been so hard for my sister to treat Samia like a daughter, seeing how much she despises the little twat!"

"Meg? Meg is Althea?"

"You aren't as dumb as you look," Nancy says.

Fire races through my veins and I do to her, something I've been wanting to do since the other night. There is no one here to save her now. I eagerly wrap my hands around her neck and snap it. She may not be Althea, but she is involved in this! She has been a key player in it all! I snap her neck with a force no living thing can withstand.

I stand over her, breathing hard, reveling in the sight of her contorted corpse. "Rot, bitch!"

Suddenly she rises, her head tilted to the side. "On with the show!" she yells, clucking around literally like a chicken with its head cut off, bumping into the building and trying to straighten up while laughing maniacally. A tattered pair of wings extend from her back as she takes flight. I watch as she soars into everything in her path, finally collapsing into the parking lot.

Her boss will have a hell of a time figuring this out tomorrow. Good.

I hop in my rental and immediately call Samia. "C'mon, pick up, pick up."

No answer.

When it goes to voicemail, I only say, "I'll see you soon, sweetie." What good will it do to warn Samia against an immortal, jealous Siren? With Nancy out of commission, she can't tip Meg off.

I take off for Bald Head Island and hope I'm not too late.

23

Léoan

When I make it to Bald Head Island, I hop off the ferry and race to Samia's house. I should have known it was Meg all along, but what twisted being adopts "the other woman"?

I leap up the front steps and find the front door open. Panic sets in as I walk inside. There is debris everywhere. Signs of struggle written all over it. When I see Finch lying on the floor of his bedroom using one arm to slide toward me, he leaves a trail of blood across the carpet.

I try to pick him up, but when I touch him, he groans. He looks up at me and shakes his head. "Samia ..."

"Where is she?" I lean down, fear setting in deeper

"Meg ... sliced me up ... took her somewhere outside ..." he wheezes. "Save her."

I run back toward the front door when I hear a voice call out from the kitchen.

"Come see what I'm cooking up in the kitchen," Althea says.

I race into the kitchen. "What have you done with Samia?"

"Nothing much," Althea says, looking every bit like middle-aged Meg. "Yet."

"Althea don't do this! Haven't we suffered enough?"

Althea leans on the kitchen island, the marble reflecting her wicked smile. "No." she shrugs. "Not particularly. You made your bed, and now you're sleeping in it." She walks in front of me. "By the way, a siren won't die unless a mortal resists them. I knew you wouldn't come back to me because of that little bitch, so I didn't even bother calling for you back in the day. I called her instead. I called her down to the water. She came because she couldn't resist as a mortal. That's when I killed the bitch and that little spawn she had growing inside of her. I cursed you as well because I still loved you and I knew I couldn't trust myself not to call on you if you were ... you. That's why I turned you into a beast of the water. I knew I wouldn't want you in the state I put you in. Sharks just aren't my type. It was for my own good."

"Killing my woman and my baby wasn't enough for you that you had to curse her, too? How much longer, Althea? How long until you get over this? I fell in love with someone else. That happens every day!"

"Not to me it doesn't!" Althea yells, her eyes bulging and her nose flaring like an angry bull. "And I didn't curse her—I only cursed you. I don't know how she gained the ability of reincarnation, but I will say that it's turned out to work in my favor. Killing her repeatedly and watching you cry by her limp body has been the absolute highlight of my existence. Her coming back as different people, and you groveling to her each and every life. You must love pain. You should have just stayed a fish, which by the way, how did you get rid of my curse? I finally get to ask you what you've done to yourself. How did you get your body back?"

"It's none of your business. Nothing I do is any of your business anymore. I just want to know what you've done to Samia!"

When she approaches me and strokes my face, I grab her hand, holding it away from me.

"Your resistance cannot kill me because you are no longer mortal," Althea says. "You're not a danger to me. Not in the least."

"For the last time! What have you done with Samia!"

"Oh, boo hoo, I want Samia, waaahhhhh!" She rubs her eyes with her fist. "Get a grip, why don't you!

I grab her by her neck and back her up against the cabinets, splintering them with her head and back.

Althea cackles and says, "Nobody hurts me and gets away with it! Nobody! I don't know what you did or what deal you struck to become immortal, but as long as I live and breathe, you two will never live happily ever after!"

I tilt her head to the side, ready to bite her neck and drain her very soul. I don't know what will happen, but at this point, I don't care. I want her gone. I squeeze her neck harder trying to choke the ever-living shit out of her. I let go when I see her smiling.

"I remember, you liked choking. Turns you on. Gets that big dick of yours hard." Althea looks down at my crotch and licks her red lips. "Maybe just a quickie, for old times' sake? Besides, you can't kill me. Oh, imagine how hot the make-up sex will be." She grabs my dick. "Will you look at that? He misses me."

I let go of her neck and back away.

"Don't want to cheat on the whack job girlfriend, huh? I get it. If she found out that you still crave me, she might kill herself like her last boyfriend did. Which is awfully funny considering that prick lived to look at himself in a mirror. I wonder if he ever told little Samia that he fucked me."

I'm tired of her talking, so I grab her and drag her across the kitchen bar, knocking everything out of the way on her trip to the edge. She fights back at me, claws forming on her hands, and she cuts me across the throat with them, leaving a large oozing gash.

I can barely fucking talk or breathe.

While I'm holding my throat, she sprouts wings, shedding her white nightgown and flying through the ceiling and the roof, leaving debris falling behind her. I run outside to see where she's going when I run smack dab into her holding her sharp talons to Samia's throat. Samia is shaking and crying.

"Léoan!" Samia cries.

Althea leaps up and flies away with Samia, and I run after her down the beach, trying to keep up.

"You can't stop what I'm going to do to her!" Althea calls, laughing. "It's fate! It's our custom!"

I hear Samia screaming, and it shreds my heart in two. I look up and see Althea circling high above me.

Althea cackles loudly—the echo surrounding me, but she won't be cackling for long, because I'm getting Samia back even if it kills me!

"That scream wasn't mine. Samia caused that herself, trying to get out of my grip. She's always been a clumsy little pain in the ass. You know, it's been fun coming up with all the cool, little ways to take her away from you time and time again," she laughs. "I wonder what I'll think of this time! I'm sure it will make a great big splash!"

Althea disappears into the night, and I fall to my knees. What can I do? Only a mortal can destroy her, and I'm not—

I'm not mortal.

Yet.

I rush back inside and stare down at Finch.

"Have you saved her?" Finch wheezes.

"I can't," I say. "But you can."

"How?"

"This is going to hurt, but I promise you'll be at peace," I say.

Finch nods. "Save her ..."

I drain Finch before he dies, and the transformation takes place. I go to the bathroom and look in the mirror at Finch, Samia's dad and Althea's lover.

I hope this works.

I run back out to the beach and shout, "Althea!"

Althea lands a few yards in front of the surf. "Finch?"

I see lacerations on Samia's face and arms, but at least she's alive. "Yes."

"But I killed you," Althea says.

"Obviously not," I say. "Let go of Samia. Now."

"But dear, we are just ... talking, taking in the night air," Althea says. "Léoan was trying to hurt her, so I flew us away. You understand, don't you, my love?"

"I heard you saying you had sex with Ace," I say. "So, you've cheated on me, and you told me you loved me. I don't ever want to see your face again! I don't want to have anything to do with you anymore. Now, give me my daughter!"

"You don't mean that, Finch," Althea says melodically.

"I mean every bit of it! I no longer love you. I want you out of my house and out of my life forever! You can't control me anymore!"

Althea looks dumbfounded and for once, she is at a loss for words.

"Let her go, Althea."

"But Finch, you ... you told me you couldn't live without me. Remember?"

"Well, I can now, Althea," I say. "I can live without you, no problem."

"But you love how I sing you to sleep at night, Finch. You love my voice. You love everything about me." She looks at me intently. "You know you love me. Come to me, Finch."

"No! Let Samia go and leave! I don't want you, at all."

"This ... can't be happening. You ..."

Althea morphs into different shapes until she's almost in her complete ancient siren form. "If you don't want to live with me, you will have to live without her!"

Althea dives into the ocean, taking Samia with her.

I run after them, jumping in and swimming to the depths until they both disappear.

I rise to the surface, gulping air and groaning. "No!" Not again!

I dive down again, looking through the murky depths, but I don't see her. I reach the surface again and let out a howl loud enough to wake up every inhabitant of the island. "Samia!"

A dog barks, and I stop howling.

I turn to see Bo swimming toward me with Samia's shirt clenched in his jaw.

I swim over to Bo. "Good dog."

Bo releases Samia. I catch her before she sinks. I swim her limp, cold, and clammy body to shore, placing her head in my lap.

"C'mon, baby, stay with me, baby," I whisper.

I put my cheek against her mouth and feel a little puff of breath. I put my ear against her chest and hear a faint heartbeat.

She's still alive! But barely.

I give her CPR, then turn her on her side as seawater pours out of her mouth. "C'mon, baby, cough or something. Breathe!"

Just then my pocket shakes and lights up like a beacon in the dark. Neptune! I reach in and pull out what he gave me—a small piece of ambrosia.

I put the fruit of immortality in her mouth and close it and hold her, hoping I'm not too late.

Bo lays his head on her legs and looks at her with mournful eyes.

"I love her, too," I say to Bo. "I have loved her for thousands of years."

When Samia coughs and spits out a little water Bo jumps up, barks, and licks her face.

Samia looks at me and smiles. "Dad? I thought you were dead. Where is Léoan?"

I look into her eyes. "I am Léoan. Your dad died so you could live." I caress her cheek. "I'll be myself in no time."

I look up to see a swarm of sharks circling something out in the water. "Oh, wow."

Samia sits up. "What is it?"

"I think it's your mom," I say. "Being devoured by some seriously ugly sharks."

Epilogue

～～～～～

Three years have passed since that fateful night on Bald Head Island. After Samia and I got married, we decided to sell the house, which Samia inherited, and relocate to Lake Tahoe—the Nevada side. There were way too many memories in North Carolina. Some good, some bad, but there's nothing like a fresh start.

Samia kisses my cheek and puts a plate of food in front of me. I eagerly dig in like never before. I no longer need blood to survive, just good old-fashioned food. Both me and Samia's curses were broken at the beach that night, but we are still immortal. I'll take it.

We get to spend eternity together.

I couldn't ask for more.

Bo starts barking. "He's going to wake up Sera," I say.

"Silly dog," Samia says. "That's okay, I have to wake her up for breakfast anyway. She might already be up."

Samia leaves to get our beautiful daughter as I dig into my plate, savoring every morsel that touches my palate when Samia screams my name. "Léoan! Come here! Right now!"

I run to the bedroom and don't see Sera. "Where is she?"

Samia points to the floor at two hamsters. One is lying injured, and an identical one sits next to it looking up at us while licking its little paws.

Samia sighs and shakes her head. "I told you that giving Sera a pet was a bad idea. Look what she's done!"

Samia sighs. "I guess now we know she takes after you. Jesus be a fence."

I hold out my hand, and the hamster crawls onto it, curls up, and falls asleep. "Well, at least she's already had breakfast. And it could have been worse, Samia. We could have given Sera a horse."

About S. Coop

S. Coop is the author of "MUTT," "My Dear Reaper," "BloodCon," "Akane," "BloodBond," "Sex, Love & Other Tragedies," "Humaning" and "Last Chance at Love" (Short Story). She currently is working on "Two Souls," which is book two of her soulmate series, and "Love in Process," her standalone romance novel.

She currently is working on **"Two Souls,"** which is book 2 of her Soulmate Series, **"Love in Process,"** her standalone romance novel, as well as **"WAIL,"** book 4 of the "Sadistic Sirens & Shrinks" series.

S. Coop is an avid collector of katanas, throwing stars, daggers, and other sharp implements of destruction.

You can interact with her at the following:

Facebook.com @ S. Coop
TikTok @ s.c00p
Threads @ scoopauthor
Visit her website @ www.scoopwrites.com

Thank you for reading!

Other books by S. Coop

MUSE
Book 1 of the Sadistic Sirens & Shrinks Series

LURE
Book 2 of the Sadistic Sirens & Shrinks Series

BAIT
Book 3 of the Sadistic Sirens & Shrinks Series

MUTT

My Dear Reaper

BloodCon
(Vampire series book I)

Akane
(Vampire series book II)

BloodBond
(Vampire series book III)

Last Chance at Love
(Short Story)